A RUNAWAY CHIMP

When I woke up, I looked around. Mush was still sleeping, but Olivia wasn't on her pillow. In fact, she wasn't in the room!

"Mush, Olivia's gone someplace."

Mush was up like a shot. "Oh no," he said. "Where could she have gone?"

I felt really scared. What if she ran into the street and got run over! What if someone kidnapped her!

We went outside and looked up and down the street. We couldn't see her.

"Maybe you should go one way and I'll go another and then we'll meet back here in fifteen minutes," I said.

"Okay," Mush said.

When I met Mush fifteen minutes later he looked discouraged. "Did you ask people?" I asked. "Had anyone seen her?"

"Not a soul ... Listen, what we better do is go back home and call the police."

A Honey Of A Chimp

Norma Klein

AN ARCHWAY PAPERBACK
Published by POCKET BOOKS • NEW YORK

With thanks to Hester Mundies whose *No He's Not a Monkey, He's an Ape and He's My Son* proved helpful in the writing of this book.

 An Archway Paperback published by
POCKET BOOKS, a Simon & Schuster division of
GULF & WESTERN CORPORATION
1230 Avenue of the Americas, New York, N.Y. 10020

ISBN: 0-671-43846-8

First Archway Paperback printing February, 1982

10 9 8 7 6 5 4 3 2 1

AN ARCHWAY PAPERBACK and colophon are
trademarks of Simon & Schuster.

Printed in the U.S.A.

IL 5+

For Ruth and Ray:
Living well is the
best revenge.

Chapter 1

"It looks kind of dingy," Mom said, looking around. She was looking at this pile of snakes that were all together, sleeping on each other's tails.

I like snakes, which I guess is a little weird of me. I really think they're beautiful. Even my best friend Nicole, who likes animals in general, can't stand them. Actually, the reason we were all at this place—Montjo's—was that Nicole came here with her uncle last month and loved it. Nicole's like me—she wants to be a veterinarian when she grows up. Only she's lucky in one way that I'm not. She has a cat *and* a dog. Her cat is named Serena. She's half Siamese and has beautiful blue eyes. Her dog is just a mutt, though. They got him from the ASPCA. His name is Blizzard, I guess because he's white. He likes to curl up in chairs. He's very smart. Nicole said she read somewhere that mutts are the smartest dogs.

My problem is my parents. My father is allergic to cats; they make him sneeze. Mom says she doesn't want to be bothered walking a dog four times a day. I've told her a million times that I'd do it, but she says dogs sometimes live to be twenty and in seven years I'll be away at college, and she'll be stuck with him. We have some goldfish, but it's hard to get that excited about fish. I mean, they're nice and I like to sit and watch them, but you can't really have a relationship with them the way you can with a dog.

Mom feels guilty about not letting me have a dog, so to make up for it she takes me to the zoo a lot. When I said Nicole knew this place that had lots of exotic animals like pygmy hippos and monkeys, she said she'd come. (She always says it isn't so much that she doesn't *like* animals—she just doesn't want the trouble of looking after them.)

We walked around some more. There were a couple of parrots in a cage. I wondered if they could talk the way they can in books. Maybe they could, but they just sat there. I guess they weren't in a talking mood.

"They're awfully mangy looking, aren't they?" Mom said.

"That's just the way parrots are," I said.

2

"I guess birds just aren't my thing," she said, gazing at them reflectively.

"Mom, what animals *do* you like?" I asked.

She thought a moment. "Platypi," she said.

I saw a platypus once at the Bronx Zoo. They *are* kind of cute, sort of like beavers up to their heads; then they have bills. "Is that all?"

"Oh, rhinos are sort of appealing," she said, "in a hard to explain way."

"As pets?"

"I wasn't thinking of pets," Mom said. "As pets—well, I just don't know. Cats would be okay if they didn't shed. I think if Dad wasn't allergic to cats, it'd be nice to have one."

"Oh Mom, look at that!"

"At what?"

"That little baby monkey . . . Oh, isn't he cute!"

We went over to look. He was a real tiny baby monkey. When we got close, he looked up at us with these big, brown eyes just like a real person. "I wish I could hold him," I said softly.

"Go right ahead," said a voice behind me. It was the tall man in the red flannel shirt who owns the store.

"Will he mind?"

"He's a she . . . That's Olivia."

"Oh." I looked down at the monkey. "How do I pick her up?"

"Here." He bent down and all of a sudden

she was in my arms. She was so soft! She had funny black hair on top of her head and big ears that stuck way out just like Grandpa's. (His ears aren't like a monkey's, but they do stick out.)

"How old is she?" Mom asked.

"Six months," Mr. Montjo said. "She's a real sweetheart . . . Not all chimps are."

"How can you tell?" Mom wanted to know.

"Same as with a baby. She's just real easy-going, likes people."

Olivia was snuggling up to me. Then she began licking my ear! It didn't hurt, it was just a funny, ticklish feeling. "I think she might be hungry," I said.

Mr. Montjo went and brought back a banana. "Here, give her this."

I offered the banana—it was peeled—to Olivia. She took it right away and began to eat it, but very daintily, not gobbling. "What else does she eat?" I asked.

"Oh, apples, lettuce . . . She's still on the bottle right now."

"Mom, do you want to hold her?" I said.

I had thought Mom would say no, but instead she held out her arms and took Olivia, who just went on munching her banana. Mom smiled down at her. "She *is* a darling, isn't she?" she said.

"I think we'll find a good home for her," Mr. Montjo said.

"Home?" said Mom. "How could someone have a chimpanzee in their home?"

"Oh, they're great as pets. You have to make them wear diapers. Toilet training them is a little complicated, but they're very bright. One couple bought one from us and raised him with their son. They said the monkey was much brighter for about a year. They were almost ready to send the chimp to nursery school!"

"My husband's a zoologist, and I'm sure he said there's a law against having exotic pets in city apartments," Mom said.

"True," Mr. Montjo said. "That law is to protect the animals. But certain people—such as a zoologist—can pass the restrictions. You wouldn't have any problem."

"Are they always so tiny?" I asked.

"This type, yes," Mr. Montjo said. "She's a pygmy chimp. They're rarer."

"Are they any different from regular ones?"

"They haven't been studied quite as intensively, but it seems they are a bit smarter and more docile, closer to humans. I think there's a group somewhere that's studying them right now, trying to test how far they can go in teaching them things."

"How did that couple manage?" Mom asked. "They must have had a big yard, I guess."

"This couple lived in the city. They had just a five-room apartment."

"So, where did the chimp sleep?"

"In their dining room, I think."

I got this sudden gleam of hope, but didn't want to say anything. I just kept looking at Olivia and she looked back at me. I could tell she really liked me, just by her expression. Mom reached out and touched her hands. "Feel how soft her skin is," she said. "It's like velvet."

"Yeah, we won't have any trouble getting rid of her," said Mr. Montjo.

On the way home on the bus, Mom looked thoughtful. "Dad should come and see her," she said.

I got excited. "Do you think he'd like her?"

"Sure . . . Well, being a zoologist."

It's true Dad is a zoologist, but the animals he does experiments with are these kind of lizards called axelotyls. When I go to visit him in the lab, they lie there looking at me with funny smiles on their faces.

At dinner we told Dad about Montjo's. "Sweetie, you should have seen this baby chimpanzee," Mom said. "She was the softest, most delicate little thing. It was incredible."

"We fed her a banana," I said, "and she ate it right up, neatly, even though she's only six months old. Her name's Olivia."

"Sounds nice," Dad said, as though he wasn't really thinking about it.

"You should come down there with us some

time," Mom said. "I bet you would be fascinated."

"I'd like to," Dad said.

"But we should go right away," I said, "because Mr. Montjo said they might sell her . . . We should really go tomorrow."

"That's fine with me," Dad said. "I don't have anything on for tomorrow."

"Do you think we could get her, Dad?" I said. "She's so nice!"

Dad frowned. "As a pet?"

I nodded. "He said they were really easy to take care of."

"Easy? Honey, he must have been joking. A chimp in a city apartment easy?"

"But Olivia's a *pygmy* chimp," I explained, "and they're very smart and very docile. Didn't he say that, Mom?"

Mom nodded. "But, Em, I think what Dad means is she may be easy for a chimp, but no chimp is going to be *that* easy . . . You'd have to toilet train her."

"So? You toilet train babies."

"Darling, listen," Dad said. "Chimps *are* very bright, for animals, I admit, but they're still very lively creatures. And they don't grow up and go to nursery school. They grow up to be big, messy, demanding animals."

"Daddy, that's not *true!*" I said angrily. "Olivia isn't messy. She's neat! I gave her a banana and she ate it *neatly.*"

7

"She's an animal, though, and there's a big difference between an animal and a person."

"Won't you even go and see her? You have all these prejudices and you haven't even seen her!"

"I said I'd go, but not to look over a prospective pet for us. It's simply out of the question."

I was quiet the rest of the meal. I kept hoping that when Dad saw Olivia he might change his mind. He can be so pigheaded at times!

The next day after Sunday breakfast we went back to Montjo's. When we got there, I got really scared. This couple was standing near Olivia's cage. "Just look at him," the woman was saying. "Have you ever in your whole life seen anything like it?"

I guess people just assume chimpanzees are boys. My heart started beating. I was scared they might buy her.

"Is that the creature you were talking about?" Dad said.

I nodded. We went over to Olivia's box. When she saw me, she lifted her arms up. "She recognizes me!" I said. I bent down and picked her up.

The couple smiled at me. "Looks like you have a friend there," the man said.

"Isn't she nice, Dad?" I said. I wished I

could give her a banana so he could see how neatly she eats. "Do you want to hold her?"

"Okay," he said. He took Olivia from me. "Uh oh," he said a minute later. Olivia had peed right on his arm!

Mr. Montjo came over. "She's a little scared," he said. "A lot of people have been coming in today."

Dad put Olivia back in her box. "How much do these animals run?" he said.

"About a thousand," Mr. Montjo said.

A thousand dollars! I thought maybe it would be a hundred or something.

"Your daughter seems fond of her," Mr. Montjo said.

"I'd say that," Dad said, smiling at me.

"It seems to be mutual," he said. "Well, chimps are like people that way. They hit it off with some and not with others . . . Of course, they tend to like children, but some of the kids we get in here come on too strong. Your daughter seems to have a nice touch with animals."

"She's hoping to be a veterinarian when she grows up," Dad said.

"*I* wanted to be one too," Mr. Montjo said. "But here I am with my store . . . It's a good second best, though."

I felt badly on the way home. A thousand dollars was so much money! "I didn't think they'd be so expensive," I said at dinner.

"The money isn't the main thing," Dad said.

"But if she was like, five dollars, then maybe—"

"Em, I said—" Dad began.

"I think we should get her," Mom said.

I looked at her in surprise.

"For a thousand dollars?" Dad said.

"You just said—the money isn't the main thing. No, I think it would be a fascinating thing for Em. She's never had a baby sister or brother and just to watch a baby grow, to help care for it . . . It would be exciting."

My heart started beating rapidly. I looked at Dad.

"But darling, listen, slow down a minute," he said. "Who'd look after her during the day? There are a lot of complications involved."

"I could take her to my studio," Mom said. "It's big . . . Look, we wouldn't have to have her forever, just for a few years, until she gets too big to handle."

"Pygmy chimps don't *get* that big," I said.

"You really think—" Dad started to say, when Mom interrupted.

"It's not for life. If she's too much bother, we'll bring her back. We're not signing our life away, after all."

"Do we have a thousand dollars?" I asked.

"We could use part of what I got for *Nesting*," Mom said. Mom is a weaver. What she makes are these things that are sort of like wall hangings and sort of like sculptures. They

10

started out not so big—more like rugs that you hang on the wall. Then they began getting bigger and bigger. Now she has a studio downtown that she shares with a friend. *Nesting* is one she worked on last year. It's kind of strange looking—like a very big, five-foot-tall, black spider with orange things coming out of where its head would be. I don't know why she calls it *Nesting*. I can never figure out the names she picks.

"Did you really sell it for a thousand dollars?" I said. I didn't want to say that I couldn't imagine someone paying that much money for something she'd made.

"Three thousand," Mom said. "Look, the couple that bought it could have paid ten. They were loaded."

"Now we have to think this over," Dad said. "It's not the kind of thing you rush into." Dad is the type that likes to think everything over. Mom says he's an "on the one hand, on the other hand" sort of person. *She's* more the kind that decides things right away. She always says that if you want to stop her from doing something, you have to act quickly because the time between when she gets an idea to do something and when she does it is not very long.

"The food wouldn't be expensive," Mom said. "She just eats fruits and vegetables."

"Where would she sleep?"

11

"He said a playpen is the best . . . We could put it in the den."

I thought Dad might object to that because the den is partly his study. He has a desk in it where he works at night. He doesn't work every night and the TV's in there too, but I still was afraid he might not like the idea.

"This other couple had one right in their dining room," I said.

"What other couple?"

"The ones who bought this other chimp. . . . They lived in New York too."

"We'd have to change a lot of diapers," Dad said.

Mom grinned. "So? We're old hands at that. . . . And this time around Emily can help us."

I've been taking a course at school on babysitting. It's for boys and girls and it's to show you how to do things like change diapers and make formula and stuff. These real mothers bring in their babies and we practice on them. I've been practicing on this baby named Jon. He's fat and kind of cute. I've gotten pretty good now, but I don't actually babysit that much because Mom and Dad don't want me to go out alone at night. They say I can only babysit in our building, and the only child on our side is Monique, who's five.

"I just want to make sure everyone realizes what we're getting into," Dad said. "We're bringing another living being into our house. It's a responsibility. It'll be fascinating, but it'll be work. Our lives will be different . . . You really want that?"

I just nodded. I had my fingers crossed as hard as I could under the table.

Mom said, "Look, if it doesn't work out, we can give her back. It's not like adopting a child. It's not for life."

I could tell it was settled.

When we got home, I called Nicole right away. She couldn't believe it. "You lucky!" she said. "When are you getting her?"

"Dad said after school on Friday. He and Mom are going to stop work early . . . See, we have to get all this stuff first. She needs a special kind of playpen with a lid on top . . . and we need to get lots of Pampers and some clothes."

"How come clothes?"

"Well, Mr. Montjo said she might catch cold otherwise . . . I guess if they're not living in the wild, they're more delicate. We might just use some of my old baby clothes."

"Can I come over and see her?"

"Sure . . . Why don't you sleep over Saturday? She's going to be in the den."

"Does she like TV?" Nicole giggled.

"I don't know. . . . Maybe we could have her watch *Sesame Street*. Chimps are really smart. They can learn words."

"We can teach her things," Nicole said.

"I know!" I said. "Dad brought home a book. It's all about this woman who works with chimpanzees and how she taught them how to do *millions* of things. They're a million times smarter than dogs *or* cats. They're even smarter than some babies!"

In bed that night I was so excited I couldn't fall asleep. I thought how lucky it was that Dad was allergic to cats and Mom didn't like dogs. Because if they hadn't been, we wouldn't be getting Olivia!

Chapter 2

On Friday when we went to get Olivia, I was so excited I could hardly concentrate in school. Mom and I sat up the night before going through my old baby clothes to find something for Olivia to wear home. We picked two stretch suits in different sizes, two undershirts and this thing sort of like a blanket with arms but no feet that Mom says is called a "bunting." Also a pink wool hat with a pompon on top. I recognized the hat from old photos of me in our photo album. We also took some Pampers.

Olivia looked a little bit scared when we started to get her ready. I made her lie down the way I do with Jon and put the Pamper on her. The six-month stretch suit fit her best, the one with the little giraffes on it. She looked cute. I thought she might mind the bunting, but she didn't. She didn't seem to like the hat, though. She put her hand up and touched the pompon and got this funny expression like she didn't know what it was. Of course, how *could* a chimp know what a pompon is?

We went home in a cab. Some people looked at us in a funny way while we waited for Dad to get the cab, but most of them smiled.

We let her run around when we got home. She makes this noise which is hard to describe. It's sort of like someone whistling. I'd thought she'd run all over the place, but she seemed sort of cautious and stayed near us. Then we took her in to show her the playpen. What we did was take a wooden pen Mom put me in when I was a baby and nail a top on it that you can lock. We shredded up some newspaper so she could make a nest for herself because Mr. Montjo said chimpanzees like to snuggle up in something at night. I got her some rubber toys at Woolworth's and Nicole gave me some old ones she had—a rubber bone, an old baby doll, and some colored balls that snap together. Mom also put in a baby blanket Grandma knitted that I used to have in my carriage. It's pale blue and really pretty.

"That's where you'll sleep," I told her. "That's your . . . house." I thought if I said "pen" or "cage" she might not like it so much.

I lifted her up and put her in. She didn't seem to mind. First she just sat there and looked around at the toys. Then she took the blanket and put it on top of her head.

"We should tell Grandma," I said to Mom. "She really likes it."

"I don't know," Mom said. "Grandma might faint if she heard her hand-knitted blanket was in a chimpanzee's cage."

Olivia began fooling around with the blanket. She put it around her shoulders like a shawl. Then she rolled it up and stuffed it into the corner. She stood up and raised her arms.

"I think she wants to get out," I said.

"Okay . . . As long as we're here to watch her, she can roam around . . . but she's going to have to learn that at night she has to stay in there."

We gave her dinner in the kitchen in a baby chair I used to have which has a table around it. We put all these things—like chopped up bananas, some grapes and some chunks of apple on the tray. Olivia picked up each thing and ate it right away. I'd thought she might not, out of being excited. That's the way I am at camp for the first few days. But she ate everything right away. When I lifted her out of the chair, she ran over to one end of the kitchen and opened the doors to the cabinet under the sink. Mom keeps all kinds of things like baking pans and plastic bowls and onions and garlic under the sink. Olivia took out an onion, sniffed it, then took a bite. I guess it didn't taste good to her or maybe she wasn't hungry since she'd

17

just had dinner—an onion isn't so good for dessert!—because she spit it out on the floor.

Dad had been watching from the doorway. "It looks like we're going to have to chimp-proof the apartment," he said. He explained how when I was a baby and I was crawling around getting into everything, he and Mom put lots of things that I could break high up. Or poisonous things I could drink by mistake.

Nicole was really excited about coming over to babysit for Olivia with me on Saturday. I should explain that Nicole and I don't go to the same school any more. Her mother decided the school I go to, Whitman, wasn't strict enough so she made Nicole switch to another school. So far she doesn't like it that much. She says the kids there are jerks. We still see each other on weekends and go ice skating and talk on the telephone a lot, though.

Mom and Dad were going out on Saturday with some friends. They said they'd pay me a dollar an hour to babysit for Olivia because if I did, it meant I'd have to turn down some other babysitting job. Really, I'd have done it for free, but I decided not to tell them that. I told Nicole I'd split it with her the way we always do when we babysit together.

Olivia seemed to like Nicole. She sat in her lap and touched her hair. Nicole has black puffy hair—it never gets messed up, no matter what. I don't know if the Afro felt good to Olivia or what, but she kept patting Nicole's head. Nicole sat very still.

"She likes you," I said.

"Gee, she's adorable," Nicole said. "I wish we could trade in Teddy and get a chimpanzee." Teddy is Nicole's baby brother. He's one and a half and a real pest as I guess most one-and-a-half-year-olds are. (She also has a brother who is four and a sister who's eight.)

Mom and Dad came in to say goodbye. They left the number where they'd be on the dining-room table. "Do you think you can manage?" said Mom, looking a little worried.

"They can call us if anything comes up that they can't handle," Dad told her.

Mom and Dad always look funny to me when they dress up to go out. They don't get really dressed up, but they wear different clothes than they do during the day. During the day, Mom wears mostly jeans and sweaters and Dad wears mostly slacks and shirts. But to go out Dad wears a regular suit with a tie and Mom sometimes wears a dress and high heels. She had on a dress I like which is shocking pink with a ruffled collar, and she was wearing this perfume of hers which I sometimes go in and try on called "Violettes de Toulouses." It's purple and it comes in a fancy little bottle. Mom said when I'm older I can wear it when I go out.

"Your father is really nice," Nicole said after

they left. "I mean, your mother is too, but compared to *my* father, *your* father is fantastic."

Nicole's father is very strict, unlike mine, and she doesn't like him at all. He works in a bank or something like that with money. Her mother is a nurse; she's really nice. They came from Puerto Rico, but before Nicole was born. Sometimes they go back to visit. Nicole said some day I could go with her.

We decided that for some reason fathers just seem to be stricter than mothers. For instance even Dad, who basically is not that strict, has all these rules he thinks I should follow. Like if I've been sick he says I can't go back to school until my temperature has been normal for one whole day, whereas Mom says I can go back whenever I'm feeling better. And with my cello Dad says I should practice an hour every day, whereas Mom says I should just practice till I know all my pieces well.

"The only thing I don't like that Mom did was to make me leave Whitman," Nicole said.

"Do you still not like it at all?" I asked.

"It's okay . . . I'm learning French which is sort of interesting. But the kids are weird. They're sort of conformists, but in this dumb way. I mean, like all of the girls are giving parties with boys and things like that."

"Well, some of the girls in our class are getting that way," I said. "I invited Lynn over last week and she said she couldn't come because she had a date with Mark.''

Nicole struck her head with her palm. "You're kidding! Mark?''

"I know. I couldn't believe it . . . Well, listen, on that night they had the potluck supper and the parents came? Sallie tried to start a spin the bottle thing on the fire escape only she couldn't get any of the boys to do it.''

"She's boy crazy," Nicole said contemptuously.

"She's still going out with David.''

"Well, he's kind of cute . . . Listen, what do we give her for supper?''

Olivia had been playing on the rug with her rubber balls, sort of batting them back and forth. I kept an eye on her while we were talking.

"Mostly she eats fruit, but Mom got some baby food she thought she might like.''

I lifted Olivia up and put her in her eating chair. Just to get her started I put a bunch of grapes on her tray. She ate them up right away.

"What do you think I should do with the baby food?" I said. "Just put it in a bowl or feed it to her?''

"How old is she?''

"Six months . . . but it's not exactly like babies.''

"Well, she'll probably make a horrible mess if you just put it in a bowl.''

"Why don't I just try it and see what happens."

Nicole watched while I put some applesauce in a plastic bowl. "Teddy used to be the worst slob you ever saw," she said. "He just smeared it all over everything—including himself."

"I know . . . I practiced on Jon, that baby in the class I'm taking? And he dumped half of it on the floor!"

Olivia seemed to like the applesauce. She dipped her fingers in and licked them off. Then she began scooping it up and putting it in her mouth.

"I guess she likes it," Nicole said.

Then Olivia turned the bowl upside down. She began smearing the applesauce all over the tray. With one finger she began to trace designs in it. "We seem to have a budding artist on our hands," I said. I was worried Dad might not like it if we made a mess, so I cleaned everything up really neatly.

"We also have a budding mess . . . Well, once Teddy poured a whole bowl of rice pudding on his head . . . Mom says that when they start to play with food it means they're not that hungry any more."

"Okay, let's take her out and give her a bottle."

"Can I?"

"Sure." I took a bottle of ready-mix formula

22

and screwed on a nipple. Then we went back into the living room.

Olivia loves her bottle. She nestled down into Nicole's arms and started to drink. "I wish I could give birth to a chimp," Nicole sighed.

"I know! Me too."

"She's so cute. Are they all so cute or is it just her?"

"I think it's partly her," I said. "I've seen lots of pictures of other ones and they weren't half as cute as she is."

When Olivia finished her bottle, we took her into the den to change her. I do it on the rug. I spread out a big piece of oilcloth first. While I did the diaper part, Nicole entertained her by dangling some rubber teething beads at her. "It's hard when you do it alone," I said. "She doesn't like it at all."

"Listen, I want to watch that special at nine. . . . Can we? Will she mind?"

"Why should she mind?"

"Well, it's her room . . . She might want to go to bed early."

"I think she can go to sleep with it on. We can turn the light off."

But Olivia stayed up to watch the special with us. It was about this teenage girl who has a baby. All kinds of bad things happen to her, but in the end it turned out all right. Olivia sat there next to us. Sometimes she got up and climbed into her cage and climbed out again—

during the day we leave the top open. But toward the end she fell asleep.

"I guess she didn't find the plot that interesting," Nicole said.

"I suppose they weren't thinking of a chimpanzee as their ideal audience," I said.

"You know what we should do?" Nicole said. "We should find a special on apes. I bet she'd *really* like that."

"They always make teenage girls so dumb on TV," I said. "They act like around six years old."

"I know! Boy, she was really a dope!"

"Her mother was awful too."

"Yeah . . . I mean, I guess if I had a baby that way my Mom wouldn't be too happy either. I don't know if she'd want me to bring it home, though."

"Well, you have so many at home already," I pointed out.

"True . . . How about yours? Would she mind? You just have you."

"I don't know if she likes babies that much," I said. "I mean, if she did, she would've had more than one."

"Listen, count your blessings, kid. You're lucky!"

"I guess . . . I used to think it would be nice to have a sister, but now we have Olivia. She's better than any baby sister would be!"

"Yeah, in theory it's okay, but then they

24

finally arrive and you have this screaming beast on your hands.''

"Anyway, the point is, Mom said she likes kids once they're older like me. I suppose she just didn't want to go through the baby thing again.''

"What *I'd* hate,'' Nicole said,'' is to have a baby, like that girl in the movie did, and then have to give it away. I'd *cry* I'd be so sad!''

"Me too! I couldn't *stand* it.''

"They'd give it to you at the hospital and it'd look all cute and everything and then some couple would just take it away and you'd never *see* it again!''

"Yeah.'' I frowned. "I hope that never happens to us.''

"It won't. We're smart.''

Nicole is always so confident about things like that. I hope she's right.

Since Mom and Dad weren't home, we stayed up to watch *Saturday Night Live*. When they did come home, we were still watching it.

"What? You girls are still up?'' Mom said, looking in the den.

"We weren't sleepy,'' I said.

"How was the little one?'' she asked.

"The little one was fine,'' I said. "She likes applesauce.''

"Good . . . I'll get some more.''

"She watched part of the show with us, but then she fell asleep.''

"Well, at the risk of being a spoilsport, I would suggest you girls turn in now . . . It's twelve-thirty."

We were both sort of tired by then so we agreed.

Chapter 3

I've learned one thing—it's hard not to be a show-off when you have a baby chimpanzee in your family. At school in babysitting class I said to Tanner, "I practically don't need this class any more, now that we have Olivia."

"Who's Olivia?" he said. He was diapering his baby, this sort of funny-looking one named Fiona.

"Our chimpanzee."

"You have a chimpanzee?" he said. "Right in your apartment?"

"Yeah, we got her last month."

"Boy." He shook his head. "Can I come over and see her this afternoon?"

"Sure," I said. Tanner's pretty nice, actually, but not as a boy friend, just as a friend. For some strange reason Mom always says that if she were my age she would fall madly in love with Tanner. To me he just doesn't seem the type anyone would fall madly in love with. He's very emotional. In gym one day we played boys against girls in a team game and he kept saying that the girls cheated because the gym teachers played on our team (it was a tie score in the end). There was a big argument and he got very upset and started crying and everything. He's pretty smart, though. (Me and him usually get the best marks on tests.) He also has this strange passion for cars. He knows practically every car that's ever existed!

When we got home, Olivia was in the den. Usually she doesn't go in her cage that much during the day, but she was there just curled up sleeping. The lid was on and locked. I guess Muriel had just left. Muriel is the woman who comes to clean our house once a week. On the day she comes—Wednesday—Mom leaves Olivia at home. On the other days she takes her to the studio. Sometimes cabs won't stop for Mom and Olivia; that gets Mom really mad. So she has Olivia wait inside with the doorman and when the cab comes, she goes in to get her. Then it's too late for the cab driver to say anything!

We went over to her. "Hi, Livvy!" I said softly.

Usually when she sees me, she gets all excited and she lifts her arms up to be lifted out of the cage. But this time she just opened her eyes and lay there.

"She looks funny," I said, starting to get worried.

"How does she usually look?" Tanner asked.

"Well, she looks pink . . . Usually she's more brown." I reached in and touched her forehead. She felt hot. I also noticed her nose was running a little. "I'm afraid she's sick," I said.

Tanner looked worried too. "You could give her some baby aspirin," he suggested.

"I don't know if chimps like that, or if it's good for them," I said. "I better call Mom."

I called Mom. She said she was about to set out anyway and would be home in about an hour.

"I hope she's not *really* sick," I said. "Like having to go to the hospital."

"Yeah, I hope not," Tanner said. I thought that was nice of him to say since he doesn't even know Olivia that well.

While we waited for Mom to come home, we played chess. I play sometimes with Dad, but I'm not that good. Tanner is very good. He won both games. Then we played Scrabble and I won.

When Mom came home, she went straight into the den without even taking her coat off. Olivia was still lying there sleeping. Mom lifted her out of the pen. "I better take her temperature," she said.

She put Olivia down on the oilcloth and took

her temperature the way she used to take mine when I was little. Olivia didn't like it. Tanner and I tried to distract her with the rubber doll, but she kept trying to wiggle away. When Mom read the thermometer, she looked worried. "It's a hundred and two," she said.

"Maybe it's supposed to be," Tanner said.

Mom shook her head. "No, I'm afraid we have a sick chimp on our hands."

"What should we do?" I asked.

"We'll take her down to Dr. Morgan . . . He's the vet Caroline uses. She says he's great."

We got Olivia into her bunting and wool hat. "Tanner, we can drop you off on the way down," Mom told him.

"Okay." He looked worried. "I hope she'll be okay," he said.

We had to wait a little while in the doctor's office. Everybody looked at us. They all had dogs and cats. We were the only ones with a chimpanzee.

The doctor put Olivia on this steel table. He began feeling her all over and took her temperature again. Then he took some stuff from her mouth and went to look at it under a microscope. "It looks like pneumonia, I'm afraid," he said.

"Is that serious for a chimpanzee?" Mom asked.

I felt really worried. What if she had something the doctor didn't know how to cure?

"Well, basically as much as it would be for a person. Her life isn't in danger. We can handle it with drugs . . . but you better leave her here a few days."

On the way home in the cab I said, "Mom, should we bring down her doll and beads? Maybe she'll miss them."

"I think if she's sick, she won't notice," Mom said. "I hope the cages there are big enough."

When Dad came home for dinner, we told him about it and he called the vet to see how Olivia was doing. "Everything seems to be in hand," he said. "They said she ought to be ready to come home on Friday . . . if she responds to the drugs."

I felt bad that night when I watched TV and Olivia wasn't there to watch with me. They even had a chimp on the show—not as the star, but in one scene. I wish she could have seen it. I've been looking for specials about apes the way Nicole said I should, but so far there haven't been any.

When I was lying in bed later I kept thinking about her being all alone at the vet's. I remembered the time I had my tonsils out and I had to stay overnight in the hospital. I hated it. I was only seven, and they wouldn't let Mom stay overnight with me. There was a boy in the room with me who kept coughing. Mainly, though, I felt so lonely and awful. Mom says I should remember that chimpanzees are different from people and don't feel things as much, but the thing is, Olivia is like a person. It's not like when people say their dog is like a person. I mean, people *came* from apes and that's a big difference.

We called the doctor every day and each day he said Olivia was getting better. Finally, Friday morning he said we could pick her up that afternoon.

Tanner asked if he could come with us when we picked her up. Mom said that would be okay.

Olivia looked fine when the doctor's assistant brought her out. She was dressed in her snowsuit and hat already, and she ran over to us. "See, usually she's like that," I said to Tanner. "She's usually very peppy and smart."

"I wonder if I could teach her to play chess," he said thoughtfully.

"That sounds a little complicated," Mom said. "Remember she's just seven months old."

"Maybe checkers?" he said.

"You know what I bet she'd like?" I said. "Chinese checkers."

Mom looked worried. "Sweetie, there's just one thing I'd be afraid of. She might eat the marbles."

"That's true," I said to Tanner. "She does like to eat things . . . but we could watch her and make sure she doesn't."

"Watch her carefully, though, and the second she eats one, stop playing."

At home, Tanner and I got out my Chinese checkers set. We didn't try to teach Olivia how to play. We just tried to show her the idea of putting the marbles in the holes. She did put one up to her mouth, but I took her hand away and said, "No," and gave her an apple instead. She sort of got the idea, but then she seemed not to be so interested any more and crawled away. So Tanner and I played a couple of games together. He and I each won once, and then we quit because he had to go home.

Chapter 4

"How was it today, Mom?" I asked at dinner.

I felt a little worried. All week Olivia has really been bothering Mom when she's trying to work. Up till now Olivia sort of played quietly or slept most of the time, but suddenly she discovered all these balls of yarn Mom uses and she began rolling them around and tangling them up.

"I don't know," Mom said, frowning. "She's really getting to be a handful."

"You know what I think," Dad said. "I think she needs more physical exercise. She *is* a chimp, after all. We have her cooped up all the time. That's not healthy."

"It's been so cold," Mom said. "I was afraid to take her out."

"Sure, but now it's March. Let's pick a nice day and take her to the park, let her run around and let off some steam."

"Maybe she misses climbing trees," I said.

That Saturday wasn't warm enough, Dad said, but he thought it would be okay if I took Olivia just to do the grocery shopping with me. That way she'd be indoors mostly. I dressed her up warm, in her snowsuit, even though it was in the fifties out. She looked cute.

In the elevator we met Mrs. Sandman. She lives with her husband on six, and they have a daughter in California who's a banker and has a basset hound. I know because Mrs. Sandman told me. She loves Olivia. It's funny. More people in our building know Olivia than know me practically. Whenever they see me, they always say things like, "How's the little monkey?" (They don't know a chimp is an ape, not a monkey.) Dad said we should get Olivia a T-shirt saying, "I'm an Ape" or "Don't Monkey with Me."

"Where are you going this fine morning, Olivia, my pet?" Mrs. Sandman asked.

People do that too. They ask Olivia questions, as though she could answer! "We're going grocery shopping," I said.

"Don't let her snitch any bananas," Mrs. Sandman said.

"She won't," I said. "She's good."

"I'll bet she is. A lot better than my grandson, Timmy. Aren't you, sweetie? Aren't you better than Timmy?"

Olivia just sat in my arms and looked at her.

I could tell she was looking at Mrs. Sandman's hat which had all these feathers sticking out. Maybe Olivia thought it was a bird.

At Food City they didn't want to let me in with Olivia. The store manager pointed to this sign, "No pets allowed. Please leave your dog outside."

"She's extremely well behaved," I said. "She's like a person."

He kept squinting at Olivia. "If she grabs any merchandise or breaks it, you have to pay for it," he said.

"I know." I bought Olivia a box of animal crackers and she ate them while I pushed her around. When we came to the bananas, I gave her one after the man weighed them and put the rest in a bag. She wasn't any trouble at all!

The next Saturday we finally took her to the park. February was really cold, but by March there were starting to be some nice days. She wore her corduroy overalls and red shirt and an old denim jacket I used to wear when I was little. I remember that jacket. I used to like it a lot. It's this very soft prewashed denim and it has two pockets where you can store up lots of things. Mom used to go through the pockets and take out some of the stuff I'd collected like old gum wrappers and used Kleenex and twigs and then I'd start collecting them again.

We took her to the Sheep Meadow. I forget why it's called that—there aren't any sheep there now. It's just a big field in Central Park where people play baseball. For gym we go there and play field hockey sometimes.

I showed Olivia a place I used to go where they have a row of swings. I put her in a swing, the kind where there's a bar to hold you in, and gave her a little push. She seemed to like it. Then I took her over to this small tree. I thought she might like to climb it since she *is* an ape.

"See?" I said, showing her. "You can climb up."

It was funny. She just sat there, looking at me as if she didn't know what I was talking about. I decided to show her. I climbed up myself. When I was near the top, I said, "See? It's fun. Do you want to come up?" I put my hands down to lift her up, but she ran off and just sat looking at me sort of suspiciously. It was strange; it was like she was actually scared of climbing a tree! I took her over to where Mom and Dad were sitting in the sun. Or rather Dad was sitting in the sun because he likes to sunbathe, and Mom was sitting in the shade, because she doesn't.

"Olivia won't climb the tree," I said.

"Maybe she doesn't know how," Mom said.

"I showed her how," I said. "But it was like she was scared of something."

"Strange," Mom said. You'd think chimps would have some innate instinct about climbing trees."

"I know!" I said.

"How do you explain it, Phil?" Mom said to Dad.

Dad had his eyes closed; you could tell he was enjoying the sun. "I have no explanation," he said. "I guess she's just over-civilized. That's always the danger when you take animals from their natural environment."

Suddenly I got worried. "Maybe she's sad," I said. "Maybe she feels like she *should* know how to climb a tree, but she just can't."

Dad looked at Olivia, who was sitting chewing a piece of grass. "I'd say she looks pretty contented," he said. "Remember, don't anthropomorphize, honey."

Anthropomorphize means don't imagine animals have feelings just like people do. I know I do tend to do that with Olivia, maybe too much.

"I think if you keep showing her, eventually she'll catch on," Mom said. She stretched. "Do you feel like playing Anagrams, either of you?"

Mom is a fiend at word games like Anagrams and Scrabble. So is Grandma. I'm pretty good, actually, and Dad is fairly good. When Mom plays Dad she always wins, but when she plays me, sometimes I win.

"We could teach Olivia," I said.

"I think it would be a bit beyond her," Mom

said, taking the Anagrams set out of her shopping bag.

In Anagrams you form words and then you can steal someone else's word if you can add one or more letters and change it. Like if someone has "scare" you can add "t" and change it to "traces." But then if they get an "r" on their turn, they can steal it back and make "craters." Sometimes you can steal words back and forth for lots of turns, making them longer and longer. The person who has the most words at the end wins. I like it better than Scrabble because you don't have to keep score as you go along.

While we were playing, Dad took Olivia for a walk to show her various things—like the people playing baseball. Mom beat me, but it was pretty close. The thing with Mom is that by the end of the game when you usually aren't paying that much attention any more, she does and will steal around six words in one turn. That's how she ends up winning so often.

"I think we should teach Olivia more things," I said, getting up. I felt stiff. "I'm going to get more books out of the library and find out more about how they teach chimps."

"You don't want her to be an overachiever," Dad said. He had just come back.

"It might be fun for her," I said. "She might like it."

"Hon, I think it's a great idea—just don't overdo it."

"Someday I'd like to take her to school and show her to everybody," I said. "Only I want her to know more things first."

"Em, Dad's right," Mom said. "Olivia's fine the way she is. Just teach her a little—don't make it a big project."

The thing is, I guess it *is* showing off but it would be so great to bring Olivia in to school one day and show the kids how she could do lots of things. I got a book out of the library and I'm going to try and teach Olivia some things. Of course, chimps are usually taught by special scientists who know how to do it. But I thought if I sort of did what they did, I could teach Olivia too.

While we were walking along, a little boy came by. He looked like around three or four. He went right over to Olivia and touched her arm. "Money," he said.

"He means monkey," said a woman who I guess was his mother.

"She's a chimp, actually," Dad said.

The boy kept stroking Olivia's arm. "Nice," he said. "Nice monkey." Then all of a sudden he bent over and bit Olivia! She gave a little cry and jumped into my arms.

His mother ran over and grabbed him. "Bad!" she said. "That is *very very* bad, Jimmy. You mustn't bite monkeys."

The little boy looked up at her. "No bite?" he said.

"No," the mother said sternly. "Biting hurts. You hurt the monkey. Now say you're sorry."

The little boy came over to Olivia. "Sorry," he said, not like he really meant it.

"Ah, the joys of having a three-year-old," Dad said after the woman and the little boy had left.

"How did we survive it?" Mom said.

"Well, Emmy wasn't like that," Dad said. "She never bit anyone."

"No, in fact there was that little boy who used to bite you, Em, do you remember? In kindergarten? Michael something."

"Vaguely," I said. I guess it didn't cause an emotional trauma or anything. I stroked Olivia. "I'm afraid she might not like coming to the park," I said. "She might remember this."

"No, she'll be okay," Dad said. "She's made of sterner stuff."

When we came to the lake, we set Olivia down again. I took her down to the water. It was pretty cold. "That's water," I said. "That's a lake—and those are ducks."

Olivia put her hand out and dipped it in the water. She seemed to like it. I guess it didn't seem that cold to her. She began splashing her hand in it.

"Maybe when it's warm, we can take her to the sprinkler," I said. "Maybe she'd like it."

Two girls who looked around six came over to me. "Is that your monkey?" the one with blond hair said.

"Yeah," I said. "She's still a baby, actually."

The other girl had brown braids. She was sucking on a lollipop. She just looked at Olivia sort of curiously. All of a sudden Olivia reached out, grabbed the lollipop and popped it into her mouth. Then she ran as fast as she could to Mom and Dad.

"Hey, listen, I'm sorry," I said. "She just likes lollipops."

"That's okay," the girl said. "I don't mind. I have some more." She took out another from her plastic purse: "You can have one."

Mom says I shouldn't eat a lot of candy, but one lollipop isn't a lot. They were the Tootsie Roll kind with chocolate in the middle. "Okay," I said.

"Mom, Olivia was bad," I said when I caught up with them. "She took this girl's lollipop."

"Well, chimps will be chimps," Dad said.

Chapter 5

March 27th is Grandma's birthday. Usually we go out to her house for the day and stay for supper. Grandma and Grandpa live in the suburbs in a very nice house. They belong to a country club and in the summer Grandpa takes me to a big pool. Sometimes I go out there for the weekend without Mom and Dad. Grandma and Grandpa don't mind if I bring a friend. Nicole has gone out there lots of times.

On the phone Grandma said she was eager to meet Olivia. "Is she very wild?" she asked, sounding a little nervous.

"No, Grandma, not at all," I said. "You don't have to worry." But after I hung up, I did start to worry a little. You see, Grandma's house is really elegant. She and Grandpa have quite a lot of money; in fact, they pay for the school I go to. Dad said that Grandpa inherited money from his father, who had some business where they made office furniture. That's what Grandpa still does. Their house is like those modern houses you see in magazines where everything goes together, only in a good way. Mom says Grandma could have been an interior decorator, she has such good taste. Grandma and Grandpa have an indoor swimming pool because swimming is the only exercise Grandma can do. Grandma got polio when she was about thirty and she has to stay in a wheelchair. It's electric and makes a buzzing sound. The doctor said swimming would be good for her heart. It's a little pool, right next to their living room. Grandma put millions of plants all around it, some standing on the edge of the pool, some hanging from the ceiling. They always keep it really warm, around 90 degrees, because that's how Grandma likes it. What I love is swimming there in the wintertime when it's cold and snowy outside. Inside it's warm and steamy, almost like a jungle with all the plants.

"Mom, what if Olivia wrecks Grandma and Grandpa's house?" I asked on the way there.

"Why should she?" Mom said. "She's not a wrecker."

"We'll have to tell them to put any really delicate things away, like those plates she got in Denmark," Dad said.

Grandpa let us in. "Welcome, welcome!" he said. He came over and hugged me. I like Grandpa a lot. He makes jokes and he's a very understanding person. My mother's parents live in Ohio so I don't see them so much. "So, this is the little lady I've heard so much about," he said, going over to Olivia. I could tell Olivia liked him. "My dear, you have beautiful eyes," he said. "Someday you're going to drive some poor fellow wild with those eyes."

Grandma was inside getting dressed, but she came out in a minute. "First of all," Grandpa said. "Today we have to celebrate."

"Happy birthday!" Mom said, giving Grandma the present she and Dad had gotten for her, a very nice ceramic casserole. Grandma likes ceramic things; she makes them herself.

"No, I didn't mean that," Grandpa said. "Today Ellen swam alone for the first time, without her life preserver."

"No!" Mom said. "How did it work?"

"Well, it was the funniest thing," Grandma said. "I was swimming back and forth, not even noticing, and I guess the thing slipped loose and came off. All of a sudden I looked down and saw I wasn't wearing it and I absolutely panicked because Sam was inside typing. And then I realized that I'd been swimming perfectly well without it. So I just stayed in my usual amount of time and that was it."

"Hey, terrific, Grandma!" I said.

Mom and Dad looked really proud of Grandma for doing that. Dad says it's very hard for Grandma to be in a wheelchair because she was very good at sports before it happened. Grandma never complains about it. She's one of these really cheerful people, not just pretend cheerful. I mean, she gets depressed sometimes, but mostly she's more cheerful than other people I know. She says it's because she comes from "peasant stock."

The funny thing is, Dad says Grandpa was almost more affected by Grandma's illness than Grandma was. He had sort of a nervous breakdown. I guess he thought it just wasn't fair. Grandma had just given birth to Dad's youngest sister, my Aunt Edith, so Grandpa had to look after Aunt Edith, Dad and Aunt Penny, who comes in between; they were just six months and three and six. For a whole year they didn't even know if Grandma would learn to do *anything* again. Finally Grandpa just collapsed. Mom says he still hasn't gotten over it. I can tell that. Sometimes when Grandma isn't around, Grandpa takes out this photo album and shows me pictures of Grandma when she was about twenty, when he met her. Grandma was really pretty then, maybe even prettier than Mom. She had black hair and a great smile with perfect straight white teeth the way movie stars have, and she had a terrific figure. "Now I know I'm not objective," Grandpa will say, "but wasn't she a beauty, Em?" I always say "Yes" and then Grandpa will say, "She still is, but then—well, I just never knew why she fell for me. When I met her at that party, she was surrounded by men. I had to fight my way through!'' He acts like he's still surprised about it!

Grandma unwrapped the ceramic casserole. "Isn't that lovely, Sam?" she said. "Look at those colors."

I gave Grandma something I made for her at school. Grandma likes birds a lot so I made her a little book called *A Book of Birds*. I had about ten pages, each with a different bird. I copied them out of a book I got from the library.

"This is wonderful!" Grandma said. "Look at this, Sam!"

"We just have a genius for a granddaughter," Grandpa said.

I know I'm not a genius, but Grandpa likes to talk that way, sort of half joking.

"How about a swim?" Grandma said. "I've already had mine."

"I might," Mom said. "How about you, Em?"

"Okay," I said. "Do you think Olivia would like to?"

"Why doesn't she come in and watch?" Grandpa suggested.

Dad said he didn't feel like it. He said he was going to play the piano with Grandma instead. Dad took piano lessons for something like twelve years when he was little; he's actually quite good. Grandma's good too. It's nice to swim and hear them playing in the background.

Olivia came into the pool room with us. She watched while I got into the pool. It's a really small pool, not like the outdoor kind some people have. It's more like a big bathtub, especially because the water's so warm. I could stay in there for hours. Sometimes when Nicole is with me, we stay in all afternoon and when we come out our fingers are all blue and wrinkly.

"It's nice," I said to Olivia. "Want to come in?" I held up my arms. I'd taken her diaper off. She just looked at me, sort of the way she looked at me when I suggested she climb a tree. "It's warm," I said. I was afraid she might think it was cold like the lake in Central Park. "It's really relaxing and nice. I'll show you how to swim."

Olivia wouldn't even come near the edge of the pool. She moved back and sat down near some plants. She touched one and then pulled off a leaf and ate it.

"Hey!" I said. "Don't do that. Grandma'll get mad. She'll give us something to eat afterward, some ice cream or something."

Mom came into the pool room. She wears an old two-piece suit she has—I think she should get a new suit. She says she should too, but she doesn't have time.

"Mom, she won't go in," I said. "She doesn't seem to want to."

"That's okay," Mom said. "Let her do what she wants."

"I think she'd like it if she tried it," I said.

"Maybe," Mom said. "But some animals, like cats, have an instinctive aversion to water. . . . Maybe chimps are like that."

I decided I would look that up in a book I have at home about chimps.

When we got out, Dad and Grandma were just finishing up. "That was good," Grandma said. "I was getting rusty."

"Get out your cello, Em," Dad said. "I want Grandma to hear us play that duet."

My cello teacher knows that Dad plays the piano so sometimes she gives me duets to practice with him. I got my cello out. It's interesting—Olivia seems to like to hear me play. Whenever I practice, she comes into the room where I am and sits there, listening. Once I went out of the room, and when I came back, she was next to my cello, looking at it from all angles, like she was wondering if it was alive. She touched it and bent down and smelled it. I wondered if she thought maybe it was an animal that made the sound.

Anyway, while I played with Dad, Olivia sat on the stone ledge of Grandma and Grandpa's fireplace and listened.

"Bravo!" Grandpa said when we were done.

"That was just lovely, Emmy," Grandma

said. "Goodness, what a lovely sound the cello makes!"

"And now for the refreshments," Grandpa said. I love having snacks at Grandma and Grandpa's house—they have such good things. Their dining room table is round and white. Usually Grandma has pine cones or candles in the middle. Once, on Christmas Eve, she bought around thirty candles and put them all around the living room and all around the pool. It was really beautiful.

Grandpa brought out around six different kinds of ice cream. They always have not just the regular ones like Chocolate or Vanilla but great special ones like Heavenly Hash or Mandarin Chocolate or Gooseberry Sherbet. And they even make hot fudge sauce from scratch and have nuts and bananas so you can make your own banana split.

I put Olivia on a chair. She reached for a banana right away. "I bet she'd like a banana split," I said. "Since she likes bananas *and* she likes ice cream." I made Olivia this really fancy banana split: first a banana, then a scoop of Heavenly Hash, then some marshmallow fluff, then a scoop of Chocolate Almond, then some hot fudge sauce, and whipped cream and chopped pecans on top and a maraschino cherry. Making it got me so hungry that I made one for myself too. Olivia really seemed to like it. She ate it backwards, though. She ate the banana first and then the ice cream. She doesn't use a spoon yet—she just dips in her hand—but she's neat. She didn't get that much on Grandma's table. When she came to the maraschino cherry, she tilted her head back and dropped it into her mouth.

Grandpa smiled. "That looks like a contented chimp," he said. "I think you've created a banana split addict."

"Isn't she nice, Grandpa?" I said. "Don't you like her?"

"She's more than nice," Grandpa said. "She's marvelous . . . but what happens when she gets big? Don't they get pretty big when they're full grown?"

I looked at Mom sort of anxiously. I don't want to give Olivia away, *ever,* no matter how big she gets. Mom said, "We'll cross that bridge when we come to it."

After snacks Grandpa took me into his study. He has an exercise bicycle in there and a jump rope. Grandpa has high blood pressure. Dad says that's partly because he worries about Grandma a lot and partly because he's a very emotional person. Grandpa is writing his autobiography. That means a story about his life. The thing is, before he went into his father's business he did lots of interesting things. Once when he was in Paris during the Second World War he met this famous Frenchman named André Malraux and they talked in French for a whole hour! And once he went down to Mexico to see this famous Russian man named Leon Trotsky, who had something to do with something that happened in Russia. I really think Grandpa's book ought to be good. I hope it's a best seller. I think he hopes so too.

He let me read the chapter he just finished. He has a great leather chair in his study with a hassock. That chapter was about when he married Grandma. It was right before the Second World War and Grandpa lived in an army barrack and Grandma had to sneak in to visit him. Grandpa loved Paris. He says that partly he wishes he had just stayed there and not gone back to run his father's business. When Dad was a teenager, he took a year off from college to go around Europe playing the guitar because he thought then he wanted to be a musician, and Grandpa says he got a vicarious thrill out of that, meaning it's something he wishes he had done.

"This is really great, Grandpa," I said when I was done.

"You really like it?" Grandpa said. He looked very pleased.

"It's so exciting!" I said. "Did Grandma really do that?"

He nodded.

I can hardly wait until Grandpa finishes his book and it's published. I'm going to go into all the stores and tell the people who run the store that it's my grandfather. Maybe I'll even bring him to school and have him autograph books!

"You know what I wish?" I said all of a sudden.

"What?" Grandpa said.

"I wish so much that Olivia could talk. . . . Because I'd like to know what she's thinking about things . . . But for some reason you can't teach chimpanzees to talk. I don't know why. You can teach them to do millions of other things—even sign language—but not to talk."

"She *is* lovely though, even if she's not an intellectual," Grandpa said. "I guess your having her makes me a great-grandfather, doesn't it?"

"That will be good when your book comes out," I said. "Great-Grandfather Writes Best Seller. . . . They might interview you for *People*!"

At around four Grandpa drove Dad to this indoor tennis court where he plays every week. In the spring he sometimes takes Grandma out on the outdoor court and she sits there in her wheelchair and tries to hit the ball back to him. Grandpa says when he sees her sitting there, he gets very mad at God for doing that to Grandma. He says he just doesn't think it makes any sense.

"I could knit Olivia a sweater," Grandma

53

said. Grandma is a really good knitter. She's knitted me a navy blue sweater and a vest with millions of colors in it. They're the kind of things you really like to wear, not that you wear just because your grandmother made them for you. "What color would she like?"

"I think she looks nice in orange," I said.

Olivia looks best in bright colors because of her brown fur; orange, turquoise blue, bright yellow. I held Olivia in my lap. Grandma measured her arms and back.

"This is going to be the best-dressed chimp on the Upper West Side," Mom said.

"Would she like pockets?" Grandma said.

"I don't think so," I said. "But it wouldn't hurt, I guess." That's the kind of thing I'd like to ask Olivia, whether she wants pockets or not. I bet she really does have a preference, but you just have to guess for her, what *you'd* want if *you* were a chimpanzee. Sometimes I think I do that pretty well, but sometimes I just can't imagine what she would like.

"Grandpa seems to be going full steam ahead on his book," Mom said.

"Well, yes," Grandma said. "I just wish he wouldn't get so depressed when it doesn't go well."

"Well, that's just the way he is," Mom said.

"I bet it's going to be a best seller," I said.

"Hon," said Mom. "You know, it's great that you encourage him, but maybe—well, you know not that many books *are* best sellers. . . . Grandpa's book might not even get published.''

I frowned. "But it's good," I said. "It's really exciting.''

"I know . . . I hope it will be a best seller too, but there are just lots of factors that go into whether a book is published. There has to be a market for it.''

"He met all these famous people," I said hopefully.

Grandma sighed. "I wish he could just write it and feel that writing it just in and of itself was worth it . . . but he's not like that.''

"No," Mom said. "He's not . . . but, you know, it's funny. *I'm* like that. When I work hard on a piece, I feel really devastated if it isn't bought by someone.''

"But that's different. It's your profession," Grandma said.

"Still . . . it's like it means all the more to Grandpa because it isn't. He's stored all this up for years and now it's pouring out.''

"I just want him to be happy and enjoy life," Grandma said. "But it's not in his nature, I guess.''

"Grandpa enjoys life," I said.

"That's true, he does," Grandma said. "You're right . . . He's just an eternal worrier.''

On the way home I sat in the back with Olivia. She fell asleep with her head in my lap.

"I think she liked Grandma and Grandpa's house," I said. "Don't you?"

Mom was trying to find some music on the car radio. She and Dad always listen to classical things. They say if I want to listen to a rock or disco station I have to do it at home with the door closed. When I watched the Grammy Awards with Mom, she kept making all these scornful remarks about the singers. "It's unbelievable. I have never *heard* such an inarticulate bunch of lyrics in my *life*," she said. "Stayin' Alive, Stayin' Alive . . . What kind of nonsense is that?"

"Mom, it's just not your taste," I said. "It happens many people like it, including grownups." Mom says she's very open-minded, but she's not about everything.

Chapter 6

I guess I am somewhat of a conformist. It's my twelfth birthday next week and I've decided to invite boys to my party. Nicole said what I should do is this—invite four girls like I usually do, and invite four boys. Then, after the boys leave, the girls can sleep over, just like last year when I was eleven.

Nicole and I decided together which boys should come. There aren't any new ones since she left last year. We decided on David, Mark, Felix and Tanner. (Tanner's real name is Richard, but for some reason he likes people to call him Tanner.)

"How about Kenny?" Nicole asked. "Aren't you still friendly with him?"

"Yeah," I said. "Only I don't think boy-girl parties are his thing, exactly."

David is nice. I guess you could say he's the most popular boy in our class among the girls.

He's sort of medium height with blond hair and he's friendly to most people. He and Sallie, this black girl in my class, have been going together all year. They go out on dates on the weekends and stuff like that. They kiss each other a lot in school. But Sallie told me she likes him more as a friend, basically.

Mark is pretty good-looking too. He's tall and he has these strange big eyes—Mom says they are "C.T.B." eyes, which means "come to bed." He's not that smart, but then none of the boys in our class are especially smart except for Tanner and John. The thing about Mark is that he goes sort of crazy every time he sees a picture of some sexy girl, like Cheryl Ladd, in a bathing suit. I think that's dumb! His parents are divorced, and his mother is this really beautiful, exotic woman with long black hair like Rita Coolidge.

Felix is okay. He's black and he thinks he's terrific. Actually he is quite good at some things, like acting. He was the lead in the play our class did last year. He played a British spy named Colonel Fitzwilliam; it was the biggest part. He, Mark and David are all good at sports. We used to have coed sports up till this year. That is, we were divided according to how good we were, not whether we were boys or girls. I'm not that good, so I was in one of the lower groups. But this year they divided it up just according to boys and girls. Mom says that's sexist and she's going to write to the principal.

Tanner is fairly bright, but also shy, sort of. I think he has a crush on me. This is why I think so. On Valentine's Day he brought in this valentine that said "To Emily." There's this other Emily in my class, Emily Horner, and everyone began asking him which Emily it was for. He said whichever of us wanted to keep it could. I said I didn't care and then Emily Horner, who's sort of aggressive, said she wanted to keep it. Then Tanner started to say "But it's really for—" and he stopped. He wouldn't tell anyone who it really was for. But I got the feeling it was for me.

For girls I decided to have, besides Nicole, Sallie, Lynn and Beryl. Lynn is my best friend since Nicole left. She lives near me and we go to school together lots of times. She has bright orange hair, freckles and is a little bit plump and slightly shy.

Beryl just came to our class last year. She can be sort of nasty at times, but not to me. She's very smart and she won this prize our English teacher, Ms. Hartwell, gave where you had to make up a Greek myth. I got second prize and Ms. Hartwell took both of us out for pizza. Beryl has braces so when she smiles it doesn't look so good, but most people like her anyway, even the boys.

Sallie is more outgoing and vivacious. Mom

says she's going to be gorgeous when she grows up. She really dresses well, not like most of us who just slop around in jeans and shirts. She actually wears dresses to school and for parties she has fancy clothes like a velvet pantsuit and a long dress with flowers all over it. When she was ten, she gave a birthday party at the Copacabana, which is this really fancy nightclub. Mom was kind of freaked out by that. She said it's very expensive. I guess Sallie's parents are quite rich. I think her mother is a model or something; that's probably why she's so pretty and why she has such great clothes.

"What about Olivia?" Mom said, looking in while Nicole and I were in the den planning the party.

"What about her," I asked.

"Do you want her to come?"

"We already have four girls," Nicole said.

"Very funny," I said. "Of course we want to have her."

"Hey, listen, I have a great idea," Nicole said. "We'll teach her to play spin the bottle."

I started to laugh. "She'd be perfect for David."

"Seriously," Nicole said. "Does she know how to kiss?"

"I don't know," I said. "But I don't want the kids to make fun of her. Also, she goes to bed around nine, usually."

"Okay, okay, it was just an idea."

This year for the first time I didn't feel like having party favors and stuff like that. I used to go out with Mom to a store and pick out everything matching—plates and cups and napkins and a centerpiece and blowers and streamers—but I think I'm sort of beyond that stage now.

Nicole said she'd bring over this strobe light she has. It's a funny box and when you turn it on, it blinks on and off. You have to turn off the lights first.

"Does Tanner still have a crush on you?" Nicole asked.

"Sort of," I said.

"He's not bad," she said.

"Yeah, he's okay," I said. "Only, not that great."

She sighed. "None of them are *that* great. . . ."

"I'll bring over some of my records . . . I have that new Donna Summer one."

"Great," I said. "My uncle said he'd lend me his Billy Joel ones."

Mom's brother, Uncle Peter, is a bachelor and he likes the same kind of music I do. He lives in Boston, but when he comes to New York, he takes me to rock concerts. Last month he took Nicole and me to the Billy Joel one at Madison Square Garden. Practically all the people there were smoking pot—you could smell it. Nicole began screaming when Billy

Joel came on. Uncle Peter says if he hadn't been deafened by the music he would have been deafened by all the teenagers screaming. Now, when he sees me, he always asks about Nicole. "How's the screamer?" he'll say. He thinks she's cute, though.

Olivia was sitting in the corner of the den, dressing a doll I gave her. It's my old Dressy Bessy and Nicole brought over some old doll clothes for it. Olivia can't put them on perfectly, like with buttons and all, but she can get them over D.B.'s head.

"Olivia," Nicole said. "All this lies ahead of you . . . When do chimps start getting interested in the opposite sex?" she asked me.

I shrugged. "I should look it up in my book."

"Are you going to fix her up when she's of age?"

"I don't know . . . I guess I don't know any other chimps. Maybe Mr. Montjo would know."

Sometimes I do worry about what will happen when Olivia gets older, if she'll be happy with us, not having other chimps for friends.

We decided the best thing would be for everyone to come around four or so. We could dance and listen to records and stuff, then stop for pizza, then dance some more. Then the boys could leave at around nine and we could stay up as late as we wanted. I asked Mom if we could stay up to watch *Saturday Night Live* and she said yes. She said we could stay up as late as we wanted since it was only once a year. I told all the girls to bring sleeping bags.

Mom and Dad gave me some nice presents. One was a diary. I've gotten lots of diaries over the years. The trouble is I tend to write in them once or twice and then forget. When Mom was a teenager, she kept a diary and she wrote in it so much! Pages and pages! Every time I read it, it inspires me. Maybe this time I'll really do it. Mom says not to worry about doing it every day, to just do it whenever I feel like it. Then they got me this great thing called "Crazy Curl" for my hair. My hair is really long now, the way I like it. It took me a little while to get the hang of it, but finally I did. When I came in after breakfast Dad said I looked like Farrah Fawcett, which I know isn't true, but it was nice of him to say.

Nicole got me what I asked her for, two records: *Donna Summer Live* and *Barry Manilow's Greatest Hits*. They're the same ones I got her for her birthday. They're really good.

Dad did fix the dining room up a little. He bought some balloons and Scotch-taped them to the ceiling. It looked nice, sort of partyish, not babyish. Mom got some paper plates that looked special but not really young like those "Super Hero" ones. Olivia loved the balloons. I tossed them to her and she tossed them back.

"I hope she doesn't get overexcited," Mom said.

"Don't worry," said Dad. "She'll be fine."

I brushed her fur so she'd look really nice and put her in her nicest pair of overalls, these denim ones with patches sewn on.

Dad began horsing around. "May I have this dance?" he asked Olivia. Then he looked at me and said, "I don't know which of these beauties to pick. How can I decide?"

Nicole came over early and helped me get everything ready.

Mom and Dad said they'd be in the den "out of harm's way." They said there was some simulcast thing they wanted to watch on TV. That means a concert that you can turn on the radio and the TV at the same time. You get really good reception that way. It was their kind of music, some symphonies by Mozart or something like that. They said they'd keep Olivia in with them most of the time.

The boy part of the party was not that great, actually. It was fair. First of all, none of the boys would dance. So we all had to dance with each other. Tanner did ask me to dance. He can't dance that well, but it was okay.

At one point Dad looked in. Olivia was with him. "How's it going?" he asked.

"Okay," I said.

"Should I go out for pizza yet?" he said.

"Sure." I was getting kind of hungry. Dad

asked everyone what kind they wanted. We ended up ordering four large ones: two plain cheese and one with sausages and one with mushrooms. I basically like the plain ones best, only with extra cheese. Grandma makes this great pizza. She gets the dough at an Italian bakery near her and then she puts in, as she says, "everything but the kitchen sink." They're quite unusual but very good.

When Mom and Dad left, things broke up a bit and some of the kids went into the den to see Olivia. I'd told them they couldn't go in earlier because I didn't want the boys to pester her. She was in her pen.

"Hey, look at that!" Mark said. "There's your date, David."

"The girl of my dreams," David said, reaching out his arms.

"Hey, take her out so we can see her," Felix said.

I said I would if they promised not to tease her. They said they wouldn't. Olivia came into the living room with us. The music was still going.

"What's her favorite song?" Felix said.

"She doesn't have one," I said.

"Does she like to dance?"

"No!" Boy, they were acting even stupider than I'd expected!

"What's her name?"

"Olivia."

"Olivia!" Felix went over and got this Olivia Newton-John record I have called *Totally Hot*. "I knew she looked familiar," he said. "Hey, babe, you can really sing."

"She's totally hot," David said.

"You better believe it," said Mark.

"Hey, guys, stop acting so immature," Sallie said. "Grow up."

Mark made a face. "Well, excuse me."

"She has a lot better taste than to dance with any of *you*," Sallie said. She's like that—she talks back to all the boys. Maybe because she's so pretty, none of them seem to mind.

When Mom and Dad came back with the pizza, we ate it on the dining-room table. The boys were hogs and had around four pieces each. I had one and a half; then I felt full. For dessert Mom did a really neat thing. There's a place called Creative Cakes where they make cakes in any shape you want, like a sneaker or a giraffe or a person or anything, only they're very expensive. Well, Mom trimmed this article out of a magazine that showed how to do it— you just cut a big piece of white cake in any shape you want and then paint icing on with a tube, like it was real paint. Mom made mine in the shape of a record. She even wrote the name of my favorite record in icing on the record. It tasted good too. She and Dad sort of hovered around. They ate in the kitchen on stools since there wasn't room for them at the table.

After we ate we played spin the bottle for a while. It wasn't so exciting. I kissed everyone and everyone kissed me. There are no great kissers among the boys in our class. There's one bad one though: Mark. He has wet lips. When it was Tanner's turn to kiss me, David said, "Aha, this is the chance he's been waiting for. Sock it to her, Tanner!"

Sallie, who was sitting next to him, socked *him* and then he shut up.

Tanner turned bright red and kissed me very quickly, like he was embarrassed.

I was glad when Dad came in at nine and said it was time for the boys to leave. I had the feeling they would've stayed all night if we'd let them.

"How come we don't get to sleep over?" Felix said. "It's not fair."

"They're afraid they'll be tempted," David said. "We're so sexy."

"Sure," Nicole said.

Once they left, it was better. We played some games and listened to records.

"Seriously, how come twelve-year-old boys are so dumb?" Nicole said.

"They develop late," Sallie said. "No, it's true. First of all, boys are generally dumber than girls. Second, they are way behind us socially. That's how come girls go out with older boys."

"Tanner just comes up to my shoulder!" Beryl said. She's five feet seven.

"Yeah, I feel sorry for Tanner and John," Lynn said.

"My Mom thinks Tanner is gorgeous," I said.

"What?" They all looked at me.

"Is she crazy or what?" Sallie said.

"I don't know. She just says one day he'll grow and she thinks he's very handsome."

"You ought to tell him," Sallie said.

"I did . . . He said, 'I'm glad someone in your family has good taste.' "

"Modest," Nicole said. "They all think they're so great, that's their trouble."

"Tanner's not like that," Lynn said. "He's nice."

"I think he's nice," I said.

"Yeah, you ought to like him," Sallie said. "Boy, does he like you!"

"I know!" Beryl said. "Did you see him blush when he had to kiss you?"

"That was just because those jackasses were teasing him . . ." Sallie looked mad. "I'm going to tell David off when I speak to him tomorrow."

"Are you still going to go out with him?" I asked.

"Yeah, I guess . . . Well, he's the best of the lot. He's kind of cute."

"They ought to clone him," Beryl said. "What are the rest of us going to do?"

At midnight we went into the den. Mom and Dad were watching TV. Dad had his arm around Mom and they had a blanket over their knees. Olivia was sleeping in her cage.

"Sorry to interrupt this cozy scene," I said.

"We get the picture," Dad said.

"How was the concert?" I asked.

"Wonderful," Mom said. "It was fantastic."

He and Mom left.

Everyone sprawled out on the floor and watched TV.

"Do your parents make out a lot like that?" Sallie said.

"They weren't making out!" I said, feeling my face turn hot.

"They were just sitting there," Nicole said.

"He had his arm around her."

"So? They're married, dodo!"

"Listen, I think it's nice," Sallie said. "My parents do it too, sometimes. In the middle of Sunday afternoon, they always say, 'We're going to take a little nap,' thinking they're fooling us. My Grandma was staying with us once and she kept saying, 'Now your parents work very hard. They need their rest. Don't disturb them.' " She doubled over laughing.

"I don't know if mine even do it," Beryl said. "Seriously."

"Oh come on," Sallie said. "They all do it."

"You don't know my Dad."

"Well, they had you, didn't they?"

She looked down. "I have this weird feeling my mother may have a boy friend."

We all looked at her. "Really?" I said. "Wouldn't your father be mad if he knew?"

"Are you kidding? He'd hit the ceiling . . . No, it was just a couple of times the phone would ring and I'd pick it up and say 'Hello' and someone would just hang up. And once I picked it up to call someone, and I heard my mother say, 'So, let's make it at one, then.' And this man who wasn't my father said, 'Okay, darling, see you then.' "

Sallie whistled. "Heavy! She'd better make sure your Dad doesn't find out."

"I hope not . . . because if they got divorced we wouldn't have any money. My father's so stingy he'd probably take all of it."

After that we watched TV some more. We slept till almost noon the next day because we'd stayed up so late.

Chapter 7

I decided to bring Olivia to school. We have a talent show every May. It's usually pretty dumb, although some of the kids are fairly talented. Beryl studies ballet. She's going to do a dance. Sallie, David and Lynn are going to do a trio. I've been teaching Olivia some things.

This book I have called *Primate Odyssey* tells about different ways people train chimps. One way is to teach them to use sign language the way deaf people do. But since I don't know sign language, I thought that might be too hard. Another way is to teach the chimp to identify words with plastic shapes. Like a blue round shape could mean apple, and a green star shape could mean banana. That sounded easier so I decided to train Olivia that way. I got a piece of clay at school and I made about twelve different shapes. Then I painted them all different colors. Dad said not to try and teach Olivia very complicated things because she's still a baby and the chimps those scientists trained were mostly adults. So I just taught her a few simple things.

I think she's really smart. Chimps are like people—some are smarter than others. I started by showing her the round red shape and saying "apple." I would hold it up and say, "Olivia wants an apple?" and give her an apple. I did the same thing with a green star shape for banana. One day I put the two shapes down in front of her and said, "Does Olivia want something to eat?" She lifted up the green star shape and I gave her a banana, and then I hugged her. I felt so proud of her! After that she seemed to get the idea. I taught her to give me a shape if she wanted something. One shape was purple and square and meant "music." If she gave me that one, I'd turn on the radio. If she gave me the yellow triangular one, I'd turn on the TV. After that if Olivia would bring me one of the clay pieces—I kept them in a basket near her cage—I'd always do the thing it meant. I also tried to teach her to do the same things herself. I'd say to her, "Olivia, I want to watch TV," and I'd give her the yellow shape. She'd go over and turn it on. I'm really glad she's so smart. It wouldn't be so much fun to have a dumb chimp.

I don't think she'll be afraid of the crowd at the talent show. I asked Grandpa when I spoke to him on the phone what he thought and he said he thought it would be okay. He said he thought maybe we should take Olivia to the zoo just to get her used to larger groups of people, but then we discovered they didn't allow chimps to visit zoos; we decided to go by ourselves instead.

When I was little Grandpa used to take me to the Children's Zoo. I would slide down the Rabbit Hole and pet the guinea pigs and stuff like that. Now I like the big zoo better. It's bigger and they have more animals. For some reason Mom and Dad don't like going there. Mom says when they were dating they took these kids she was babysitting for to the Bronx Zoo and Dad ended up getting mononucleosis. I don't think that has anything to do with the zoo, but I guess they have some kind of bad memory of it.

One thing I noticed this time was that the Monkey House wasn't that nice. It's sort of smelly and not that great-looking. I wouldn't want Olivia to ever have to be in a zoo. It's awful to think of her being caged up all the time.

"See," I said, pointing to a chimp crouched in a corner. "That's what Olivia'll look like when she's grown up."

"Nonsense," Grandpa said. "Olivia will be much handsomer than that forlorn creature."

In the cage there was this mother chimpanzee

named Sasha and her baby who was named Kenya. Sasha came over and looked out at us.

Her baby kept following her everywhere. He had a banana that he held, but didn't eat.

Then the keeper came along.

"I have a chimp for a pet," I said. I explained about how we got her.

"What are you going to do with her when she's full grown?"

"Nothing," I said, defensively. I get worried when I think about that.

He shook his head. "It'll be a little tricky having a full-grown chimp in a city apartment," he said.

"No, it won't," I said. "It won't be! We'll just make her a bigger cage."

"It's not fair to the animal, really," he said. "They need companions of their own breed."

Afterward when Grandpa and I were having lunch at the cafeteria, I asked him if he agreed with the zoo keeper.

"Well, I'm not an expert on it, Em," he said. "But there does seem to be something in what he said."

"Yeah," I said. I felt really bad. "I think *I'm* a good companion for her," I said.

"Of course you are," Grandpa said. "But perhaps they play with each other in a special way that we don't understand."

"She wouldn't fit *in* with regular chimps," I said. "She's used to being with people. She'd hate it. Look how old and smelly the cage was."

"Well, there are all different kinds of zoos," Grandpa said. "Some are modern and allow the animals more space to roam around."

I sighed. "I don't know . . . I hope we can keep her. I think she is going to be small for her age."

Grandpa was sort of poking at the seven-layer cake he'd gotten for dessert. "Can I have it?" I asked.

"Help yourself. I have to warn you—I think they've glued the layers together with rubber cement."

Grandpa is sort of a gourmet. He doesn't like junk food at all. He took this jar of pignolia nuts out of his pocket. "Have some pigs," he said.

I asked him if Grandma was still swimming around the pool without her life preserver. He said she was. "Brave little girl," he said. I thought that was funny since Grandma isn't exactly a little girl. "She's got more gumption than anyone you'll ever meet."

"How is your book coming, Grandpa?" I asked him.

"Pretty good," he said. "Of course now that the war is over, it's not so exciting . . . and then the part about Ellen's illness is hard to write. It's sort of like living it all over again."

"Do you believe in God?" I said. I know

Mom and Dad don't, or at least they don't go to church, although Mom did when she was little.

Grandpa frowned. "I used to think I did," he said, "but after this thing with Ellen . . ." He smiled in a painful kind of way. "All I can say is he's got a lot of explaining to do if I get a hold of him."

We walked all around the zoo. "Do you think it's showing off to bring Olivia to the talent show?" I asked Grandpa.

"No, in what way?"

"Well, showing her off."

"But you've trained her. You should be proud of that."

"Yeah, but maybe I should have just done it for its own sake, not to show off to people about it."

"Em, just say your motives are mixed, like most people's."

That made me feel better.

The funny thing is I never wanted to be in the talent show before. Dad used to ask why I didn't play my cello, but I always thought it would make me feel awkward going up and doing that. I just can't imagine how Beryl can get up and dance that way. But then I guess if you're going to be a dancer, you have to get used to people watching you do it. Dad says for true performers that's a turn on, being watched. I guess I must not be a true performer.

This year, to celebrate Schubert's birthday, my cello teacher had some of his students come over to his house. Everyone played one piece by Schubert that they had learned. I'd practiced mine a lot so it went okay, but I felt really nervous; my hands were all sweaty. At my next lesson my cello teacher said I did okay. He said once he was giving a concert in somebody's home and one of the strings of his cello broke. He had to go off and fix it and then come back, right in the middle of the piece!

The day of the talent show I had to get everything ready. I'd practiced for Mom and Dad a few times; it seemed to go okay. First, I gave them the little speech I'd prepared about how we got Olivia. Then I showed the clay shapes and explained how I trained her. Then I told Olivia to do various things and she did them.

Mom drove me to school with Olivia. "Mom, I feel really nervous," I said, scrunching down in my seat.

"Don't be, honey," Mom said. "It'll go fine."

I'd told Mom and Dad that I'd rather they didn't come. They've seen it already and it would just make me nervous if I saw them in the audience. Actually, I wear glasses for things that are far away like movies, but I decided not to wear them for the show. That way I won't be able to see the faces in the audience that well and recognize my friends.

Grandma and Grandpa said they wanted to come. I said they could. I told Mr. Kelly, our teacher, ahead of time so he would know about Grandma's wheelchair. She can get out of it and sit in a regular chair like they have in the auditorium. Grandpa folds up the wheelchair and puts it away.

Luckily, I wasn't the first one on the program. Some people actually *wanted* to go first because they said then it would be over with sooner. I didn't want to go last because then I'd spend the whole time worrying about my part and not be able to concentrate on the rest of the show, but didn't want to go first either. They put me in around the middle.

Beryl was first. She did her dance. It went really well. It was a modern dance. She wore a bright blue leotard. The prettiest thing about Beryl is her hair—it's very light blond, almost white. She had it in a pony tail and every time she'd whirl around, it would sort of flow out like a scarf. You couldn't tell she wore braces because her mouth was shut. I was really impressed. When I was around seven, I used to take dancing lessons at a place in Carnegie Hall. But I wasn't that good and I never liked it much. Mom says I'm basically a head person like her and Dad. She says there are head people and body people and that body people are naturally good at things like dancing. I guess Beryl must be both because she's smart too.

Then Mark did his imitations. This year he did Jimmy Carter, James Cagney and Roseanna Roseannadanna. He can really change his voice to sound like different people. He's surprisingly good.

Sallie did a singing thing with her two sisters. She has one older sister, Marie, who's in eleventh grade, and a little sister, Gigi, who's in third grade. They all came out in fancy dresses wearing a lot of makeup, even Gigi, and they sang a Donna Summer song called "Last Dance." Actually, Sallie can't sing that well and neither can Gigi, but Marie can. Sallie looked terrific and wiggled around just like a real singer. Everyone applauded a lot for them.

Then it was my turn with Olivia. I brought the things I needed on stage—the fruit, the TV, the radio and my basket of shapes. I told Olivia to sit in a chair. Olivia wasn't at *all* nervous— of course she didn't know what was going on, which I guess makes a difference. Evidently seeing a lot of people didn't mean that much to her. At the beginning I felt really scared. When I got up to make my speech, my voice cracked. I had to clear my throat and start again. Luckily, I didn't forget what I was going to say. What I was really afraid of was that Olivia wouldn't do the things the way she did at home. But she did! She went right over and turned on the TV when I told her to and even stood there and watched it for a little while until

I told her to turn it off. She brought me an apple from the box when I showed her the blue shape. She did everything just right. At the end everyone clapped and clapped. I could see Grandma and Grandpa sitting toward the back. I could hear Grandpa yell, "Bravo!" and "Encore!"

But I felt really relieved that it was over. When I went off stage my heart was beating so fast I practically thought I was going to faint. Olivia curled up in my lap and watched the rest of the show with me from the side of the stage.

"Well, I think we have a natural actress on our hands," Grandpa said when he came up with Grandma after the show.

"Who?" Grandma said. "Emmy or Olivia?"

"Both," he said.

Grandma said she thought I had a lot of talented people in my school. She said she liked Beryl's dance a lot. Grandma likes modern dancing and she goes to a lot of dance shows. Grandpa said he liked Mark's imitations.

Then this funny thing happened. I was standing around talking to Grandma and Grandpa when this man came over to me. He said he was David's father, Mr. Beiser, and he worked for a television station. He wanted to know if I wanted to appear with Olivia on this show for children that they put on in Boston called "Pizzazz." It's taped ahead of time and they sometimes have segments where they show kids who do unusual things. I said I'd have to ask my parents.

"You see?" Grandpa said. "Just as I expected. The two of you will end up in Hollywood before the year is out."

"Grandpa, come on," I said.

"Olivia, you're going to be a star," Grandma said. "What do you say to that?"

Olivia was just sitting on the table, eating a banana.

"She looks singularly unimpressed," Grandpa said. "A most blasé young chimp. . . . My dear," he went on, going over to her, "what you need is an agent. I want to offer you my services. With a little help you can be propelled into the front ranks of animal actresses. You have immense natural charm, beauty and grace."

"Sam, remember it was Emmy who taught her all those things."

"Am I denying that?" Grandpa said. "I give full credit to Emmy."

That night Grandma and Grandpa took Mom and Dad and me out to dinner. We asked Tanner if he would babysit for Olivia; he said yes. We went to this restaurant that Grandpa likes called The Russian Tea Room. The waiters wear funny costumes and it's always decorated like it's Christmas. Grandpa likes to order strange things like calves' foot jelly. I always order something called blini which are these pancakes with red caviar inside. Mom always orders Chicken Kiev. When you cut it open, butter spurts out. It's yummy.

I told Mom and Dad about David's father. I asked if I could be on the show.

Dad looked worried. "Do you want to, Em?"

I nodded.

"Well, I suppose I could take a day off and go down with you."

"Em can manage by herself," Mom said. "Let her fly. Peter can meet them at the airport."

I was beginning to get really excited. "Would they let Olivia sit with me?"

"We'll have to check on that," Mom said. "After all, it's not the same as taking a baby."

Chapter 8

Uncle Peter is a poet. He's had lots of poems published. He always sends us copies of the magazines his poems are in. I don't always understand them, but if I ask him, he explains. He doesn't mind if you ask him. Writing poetry doesn't earn you that much money so last year he got a job as a chef. He lives in the home of a terribly rich couple in Boston—they earn around fifteen million dollars a year!—and cooks for them. It's a really fancy house. Once, when they were away on vacation, Mom and Dad and me came down for the weekend. We ate dinner in this enormous dining room with paintings called frescos on the walls. Uncle Peter made a fantastic eight-course meal: chestnut soup and roast pheasant with apple prune stuffing. For dessert he made a strawberry soufflé. He says he likes to make "challenging

things." For Christmas he gave himself a Cuis-
inart and he loves to use it.

What's sort of sad is that this couple, the
Radins, don't really appreciate Uncle Peter's
cooking. Mrs. Radin is always on a diet. At
night she sneaks into the kitchen and eats taco
chips. Mr. Radin has an ulcer. Once Uncle Peter tried to quit—he thought maybe he ought
to do something else—but the Radins kept calling him and begging him to come back. They
said they couldn't live without him. So he came
back. The Radins are so rich they have lots of
other servants too. It's sort of like *Upstairs,
Downstairs*. I never knew there were people
who really lived like that any more. There's
someone who cleans and someone who does
all the shopping. The other thing Uncle Peter
has to do besides cook is walk their dog, Sebastian. Sebastian is a special kind of dog called
a brindle Great Dane. He wears a muzzle when
he goes out because he used to bite other dogs.
Uncle Peter doesn't like him very much. But
in between cooking and walking Sebastian he
has lots of free time to write poetry.

Uncle Peter said he'd be glad to meet me at
the airport. He said he didn't mind having Olivia at the Radins' house since they were in
Jamaica, but I had to swear I'd watch her like
a hawk and not let her touch any of their frescos. They're worth around a hundred thousand
dollars each, so obviously the Radins would be

mad if anything happened to them. I think it would make me nervous to have such expensive things in my house, but I guess the Radins don't mind.

We checked all the airlines, and only a small commuter line said I could take Olivia if I held her in my lap. I said I would. Mom said I should wait till school was out since it was almost June.

On the airplane I sat next to a fat man who read the newspaper most of the time and a woman who was about twenty-five years old. The woman liked Olivia a lot. She said she was a science teacher and she loved animals. I let her hold Olivia. I explained about the show. She said she would tell her niece, who is ten, to watch for me.

When we got off the plane, I saw Uncle Peter right away. I always call Uncle Peter "Mush." I don't know why. I started calling him that when I was little. Mush is almost bald which Mom says is strange because her father has all his hair and he's sixty-two. Mush wears glasses and is quite thin. He's two years younger than Mom which makes him thirty-five. I thought of introducing him to Judy, the teacher I met on the plane, but he's gay and likes men better than women, according to Mom, so I didn't. Mom says that her mother, my Grandma May, is always saying, "Why doesn't Peter meet some nice girl?" She says that some Christmas she's going to yell, "Because he doesn't want to! He's gay!" But so far she never has.

"So this is the famous Olivia," Mush said. "Welcome to Boston."

Mush was wearing a seersucker suit. He also wears gold-rimmed aviator-style glasses. I think he's nice-looking, even though he's bald. He's very neat and he wears expensive shirts made by famous designers like Pierre Cardin. He even has nice shoes. They're always polished. You notice what he wears, unlike Dad, who wears the same thing most of the time.

"She had a good time on the airplane," I said. "Nobody seemed to mind."

"Well, it's not often they get a TV star, I bet," Mush said.

Mush has a car. It's a silver BMW. He likes expensive cars. Tanner would go crazy over the car. It *is* kind of jazzy looking. He has a great stereo in it with speakers and this thing for cassettes.

"Have you heard the new Linda Ronstadt?" he asked me.

"Yeah, it's okay," I said. I sank back into the bucket seat. It was really comfortable.

"What are Olivia's tastes in music?" he asked.

"Well, she likes most things," I said. "She definitely likes music." I told him how I'd shown Olivia how to turn on the radio and how sometimes I'd come into the den and she'd have it on. I put it near her cage so she could turn it on when she was in her cage.

The show wasn't until Saturday morning. Olivia seemed very tired and fell asleep while Mush was cooking dinner. He said that was good because it would make him nervous to have to watch her while he was cooking.

He made a Chinese dish with chicken and cashew nuts and scallions. It was great. Maybe when I'm older I'll take cooking lessons from Mush. Neither Mom or Dad is that great at cooking. They can both do regular things like meat loaf and steak, but not fancy things. Mom can do two fancy things—coconut cake and chicken cacciatore—and Dad can do crepe suzettes and leg of lamb with coffee poured over it. But that's all. I like to watch Mush cook. He cuts things up very neatly and he cleans up after each step, unlike Mom and Dad who tend to leave a mess till the end.

"How about a little wine?" he said when we were ready to eat. We ate in the kitchen, not in that fancy dining room where we ate with Mom and Dad.

I said I'd rather have Coke, but Mush said having Coke with a fine meal was a travesty. He said I could have water if I wanted, so I did. I love the Radins' refrigerator. It has a thing on the outside that you can press and crushed ice will come out! I wish we had a refrigerator like that. It must cost a lot of money, though.

"I'm really getting into Chinese cooking," Mush said. "It's not so fattening which pleases Mrs. R., and it's low in cholesterol which pleases Mr. R." Mush calls the Radins Mrs. R. and Mr. R. most of the time. He doesn't like it that Mr. R. won't eat butter. Mush says all great cooking is based on butter. He doesn't approve of margarine, but to please the Radins, he uses it sometimes.

"How come they're in Jamaica?" I asked. It seems like the Radins are on vacations practically all year round.

Mush explained that Mr. R. makes his money selling paintings to other rich people so he doesn't have an actual office where he goes every day. That's why he can take lots of vacations. "It's fine with me," Mush said. "I can write more when they're gone."

Even when Mush eats just by himself, he makes gourmet foods. He says he doesn't see the point in eating anything *but* good things. He says it would be a waste of time.

In his bedroom he has a picture of me and a picture of Olivia that I sent him. It's a small room. I think it's sort of mean of the Radins to give Mush such a small room, but he says that after all he *is* a servant to them. *Their* bedrooms are huge. They each have their own bedroom; Mush said rich people sometimes do. Mrs. Radin has a room like the ones you see in magazines. It has a fourposter bed and a white comforter with little rosebuds on it. There are big curtains around the windows in the same material. In the bathroom the shower curtain is made of the same material too. So is the wallpaper. I guess she must like that design a lot. She even has soap that matches it. Mr. Radin's bedroom is completely different. His bed is made of stainless steel. His room looks sort of like those dens you see in pictures. He doesn't have a moose head on the wall, but it's that kind of room. He has a pipe rack with dozens of pipes in it and a big carved wood dresser and a Persian rug that Mush says is worth "an arm and a leg." Mush says the Radins have very conventional tastes and don't know how to spend their money properly. "Basically they're Philistines," he says. I looked that up. It means members of a non-Semitic people who settled on the coast of Palestine in about 1200 B.C. It also means people who don't have good taste.

I know what Mush means, but I sort of like Mrs. R.'s bedroom. She has this bureau with around thirty drawers. Each drawer is lined with sweet-smelling paper. Everything is so neat! She has all her sweaters lined up according to color—all the orange ones in one pile and all the blue ones in another pile. She has around a *million* sweaters. In her closet she has a special rack for all her shoes—she has around a million pairs of shoes too. She has the kinds of shoes you see in magazines but you don't imagine anyone actually wearing—like purple satin sandals and green boots with fur on top, *real* fur.

I doubt I'll ever be really rich like the Radins and, even if I was, I don't think I'd fix my house up the way they have. What *I'd* do is buy a big house in the country with lots of land. I'd have horses and cows and chickens and pigs and dogs and cats and different kinds of apes. If I get married, I'm only going to marry someone who loves animals. I don't care what he looks like or anything else, but I couldn't marry someone who didn't love animals.

Mush said I could sleep on the bed and he would sleep on the floor on the air mattress he has. I said I didn't mind sleeping on the air mattress but he said it was important to get a good night's sleep since I had a big day ahead of me. We put Olivia on a big pillow in the corner.

I slept really well. I don't have trouble sleeping in strange places the way some people do. When I woke up, I looked around. Mush was still sleeping, but Olivia wasn't on her pillow. In fact, she wasn't in the room! We'd closed the door, but I guess she'd opened it.

I gave Mush a shove. "Mush, Olivia's gone someplace."

Mush was up like a shot. "Oh no," he said.

"This is all I need. Where could she have gone?"

We ran all over the Radins' house. It's a five-story brownstone and has a lot of room. I was scared Olivia might have run into Mrs. R.'s bedroom and lain down on her comforter. "Will they fire you if they find out?" I asked Mush.

"It depends on what she does."

I felt really scared. I kept thinking of all those *Curious George* books I used to like when I was little and all those horrible adventures he got into, like grabbing on to a bunch of balloons and floating way up in the air. Of course, monkeys are more mischievous than chimps, but still. What if she ran into the street and got run over! What if someone kidnapped her!

I started to cry. "I'm so scared, Mush."

"Sweetie, don't be. We'll find her."

We went outside and looked up and down the street. The Radins live on a small side street with a lot of trees. We couldn't see her.

"Maybe you should go one way and I'll go another and then we'll meet back here in fifteen minutes," I said.

"Okay," Mush said.

I went all down the street, looking in all the side alleys and gardens. At the corner I saw a newsstand. There was an old man sitting in back of it. "Did you see a monkey come by here?" I asked.

"What kind of monkey?" he asked suspiciously, like he thought it was some kind of joke.

"A chimpanzee, actually," I said. "She's small and has dark brown fur."

He shook his head. "Naw, I didn't see anything like that."

When I met Mush fifteen minutes later he looked discouraged. "Did you ask people?" I asked. "Had anyone seen her?"

"Not a soul . . . Listen, what we better do is go back home and call the police."

The police! All the way back to the Radins I kept worrying about what had happened to Olivia. What if she'd gotten into some terrible trouble that would cost Mom and Dad lots of money? Lately whenever anything happened with Olivia, even some little thing like her fooling with Mom's yarn, she or Dad would start saying things like, "She's getting to be a real handful" or "A child would know better than to do that."

But when we found Olivia, she hadn't gotten into any trouble at all. She was in the upstairs living room with Ms. Bletter, who does the cleaning. Maybe Ms. Bletter reminded Olivia of Muriel, who cleans for us. Ms. Bletter is white and Muriel is black, but they're both about sixty and a little bit plump. The other difference is Ms. Bletter wears a uniform and Muriel just wears regular clothes. Anyway, Olivia was standing there holding this blue feather duster while Ms. Bletter was running the vacuum cleaner. When she saw us, she turned it off.

"How do you like my new helper?" she said to Mush. "This is just what I need. A nice, friendly, efficient girl to give me a hand."

Mush sat down in one of the chairs. He looked pale. He put his hand on his heart. "When did you find her?"

"Oh, just as I came in, there she was in the kitchen, looking for something to eat, the little lamb. I gave her a banana and changed her. I hope that's okay?" she asked me. "Now, we're old pals. She likes the vacuum. I would have let her work it, but I was afraid Mrs. R. might object."

"She didn't . . . destroy anything?" Mush asked nervously.

"Not a thing . . . So, when does the show start?" I guess Mush had told her about Olivia and me.

"At eleven," I said. "They're just taping it."

"Give them both a good, hearty breakfast," said Ms. Bletter to Mush.

"I will," Mush said.

We took Olivia back to the kitchen. At home I don't have much for breakfast, just cereal, since that's what Mom and Dad have. Mush just wanted a croissant with half of a pink grapefruit and a cup of black coffee. I added a little coffee to a cup of milk and put in heaps of sugar. That way it tastes like a coffee milk shake. I had a pink grapefruit too and then a bowl of this great Granola which Mush makes especially for Mrs. R.—Olivia had some Granola too; she seemed to like it.

I got sort of dressed up, for me, for the TV show. Mom said I should. She said since it would be in color, why not wear bright colors? She likes bright clothes anyway. She bought me these bright red overalls at Bloomingdale's and a yellow velour top. It looked good. Mush said I looked very snazzy. "If you look like this at twelve, what are you going to look like at sixteen?" he said. "You'll be knocking them dead."

Unfortunately, I haven't met anyone yet I *want* to knock dead, but I guess when I do, that will be helpful. I dressed Olivia in bright yellow corduroy overalls and a red shirt so we'd match. Mush said he thought that was excusable for a TV show.

He drove me to the studio. He'd brought along his camera and said he'd ask if he could take pictures. The producers were this young couple who were married to each other. He was white and she was black. She looked sort of like my fifth-grade teacher, Ms. Jenson. She had the same round granny glasses and this soft Southern voice. She said she came from Kentucky. He was just regular looking. He had curlyish brown hair and was wearing blue jeans and a checked shirt.

There wasn't any audience. It was just me and Olivia on this stage with a backdrop painted with big stripes and the word *Pizzazz* written in big purple letters.

"I love your outfit, honey," Jill said. That was the producer's name. She said I should call her Jill. "Don't you, Jim?"

"The colors are perfect . . . Does Olivia usually wear clothes?"

I explained that we'd been afraid that Olivia would catch cold without clothes, but now that it was warmer, it was partly to keep her diapers on.

"I'll tell you what," Jill said. "Why don't you start off telling us some of that, how you came to get Olivia and what it's like taking care of her."

"She got sick once," I said. "Should I tell about that?"

"Anything that seems interesting to you. After all, most kids are never going to have a chimp as a pet. They'll really be curious."

"Why don't you tell about this morning?" Mush said.

"What happened this morning?" asked Jim.

I told him about how Olivia had gotten loose and how scared I'd been that she might have been run over or something.

"Great," Jill said. "Start off with that . . . What do you think, hon?"

"Okay . . . We want to leave time for the part where you show what you've taught her."

We practiced once. I'd thought I would be nervous, but I wasn't. Partly, it helped that there was no audience and that Mush was there. In some ways it was a lot less scary than being on stage at school where there were so many people and you could see all your friends and Grandma and Grandpa and everyone. I was glad they let Mush take photos because then I'll have a record of what happened. I have a scrapbook of Olivia with all the photos of her I've taken since we got her—one when we were picking her up at Montjo's, and another when we took her to the park. You can tell from looking at the photos how she's changed. She was really tiny when we first got her. She's not huge now, but she's definitely bigger and has more fur.

After the show, the producers took us out to lunch. They said it was okay if Olivia came. It was a health food place which I knew Mush would like because everything was fresh and everything looked pretty. Mush says the aesthetic effect of a meal is almost as important as the culinary effect, which means it should look good *and* taste good. Jill and Jim said they hadn't been married when they began to produce the show, but they got along so well, they decided to get married. You could tell they really loved each other, like Mom and Dad. She kept rumpling his hair and calling him "Honey" and he kept reaching out and holding her hand under the table.

They said they weren't sure when Olivia and me would be on, but they'd let us know. After lunch Mush drove us to the airport.

"They were nice," I said.

"Yeah," said Mush, sort of sadly. "They're lucky."

"In what way?" I asked. I was surprised Mush thought they were lucky because Mom always said he didn't want to get married to anyone because of being gay.

"Living with yourself can get kind of lonely. It must be nice to have someone living with you," he said.

"You can live with just a friend," I said, "just somebody you like." That's what I'm going to do until I get married. I don't think I'd want to live alone.

"I guess I don't know anyone I like that much," Mush said.

That sort of surprised me. I know I would like living with Nicole. That's what we're going to do. We're going to go to the same college and get an apartment together. I think we'll get along really well. The only thing is, she's quite messy and I'm fairly neat, but Mom and Dad are like that—she's neat and he's messy. Mom says if the neat person can just not bug the messy person too much and the messy person can occasionally clean up a little bit, it works out.

"Don't you know anybody from school?" I said. "Or, like, somebody who writes poetry?"

He shook his head. "Not really . . . I mean, I know people, but no one I'd like to live with."

"Maybe you're not the type to get married," I suggested. "Not everybody is."

"Maybe." He pulled into the parking lot. "I think I would like having a child."

"Well, you could adopt one . . . You can do that even if you're *not* married. That's what I'm going to do if I don't find somebody I want to marry."

Mush turned off the motor. "It seems like such a big responsibility. I don't earn that much money . . ."

It's true. Mom said children are very expensive these days, especially if you send them to private school. I guess that's one reason I'm an only child. "Maybe someday you'll write a poem that somebody will buy for a lot of money," I suggested.

Mush shook his head. "Poems never sell for a lot of money."

"Maybe you'll become a chef at a very fancy restaurant and invent something like peach melba."

Mush smiled. "Maybe," he said.

He handed me Olivia. She was sleeping in her basket in the back seat. I was glad we had such a serious talk.

At the gate Mush kissed me goodbye. "I'm really glad you came, Emmy," he said.

"Me too," I said. Olivia reached out and touched Mush's arm. "See? She likes you," I said.

"I like her," Mush said. He stood and waved even after we got on the plane. I held Olivia up to show her where he was, but I don't think she understood.

When I arrived at La Guardia, Mom was there to pick me up. She asked how it went. I told her fine. I told her about how Olivia got loose and about Ms. Bletter and that couple who produce the show and about Mush's wanting to get married.

"How come he does?" I said. "I thought you said he was gay."

"He's ambivalent," Mom said. She explained that meant you can feel two different ways at the same time.

"If I ever get rich," I said, "I'm going to give him a lot of money. Then he can adopt a child."

Mom said she thought that was a good idea.

Chapter 9

The kids at school were really curious about how the TV show had gone. Our core teacher, Mr. McCormmach, asked if I'd give a class report on what it had been like. I did and then someone asked when it would be on the air. I gave the date they'd told me—May 3rd. Everyone said they wanted to watch.

The week of May 3rd one other exciting thing happened. Tanner asked me out. He asked me if I wanted to go bowling with him on Saturday. I told him I was terrible at bowling. He said that was okay.

I guess this is my first date. Lots of girls in my class go out, not lots but some. Sallie, of course, goes out with David, and Lynn sometimes goes out for pizza after school with Mark. I guess no one I know is really in love with anyone, not yet. I'm certainly not in love with Tanner! He's okay, though. I think I might get better at bowling if I did it more. I'm basically not that good at sports. Also I'm sort of lazy. Mom says in the summer I should get a tennis permit and play in the park with Nicole. I might. She's not that good either so it would be even.

Mom said that she and Dad would stay home and babysit for Olivia. Sometimes they go out Saturday night, but this time they weren't going to. Dad had some work and Mom said she had a book she wanted to read.

"I remember my first date," Mom said. It was dinner time and we were just finishing. "It was with this pathetic, lonely creature named Sylvester Lieberman. He was the editor of the school paper the year before I was."

"What was so pathetic about him?" I asked.

"Oh, he just had a forlorn air," she said. "You know the type."

Maybe he was like this boy in my class, Paul Chermeyev. Nicole once said Paul looked like Lincoln a week after he was shot. That's not a nice thing to say, but I know what she meant.

"Where did you go?" I asked.

She frowned. "Where *did* we go? I just can't remember. To a movie or something. I remember he tried to kiss me and I didn't want to so I bent down to tie my shoe."

"Mom! What a weird thing to do!"

Mom smiled. "Yeah, it was weird . . . Well, I was a strange girl in some ways."

Dad was making chocolate sauce to pour

101

over vanilla ice cream. He's shown me how to do it. You just add sugar, water and butter to chunks of semi-sweet chocolate. It's so good!

"What was *your* first date, Dad?" I asked, watching him add the sugar.

"Let me see . . . It was with a girl named Helen Montgomery."

"Who was she?"

"Well, it was a blind date, actually."

"Where did you go?"

"We went to the Stork Club."

Mom let out a shriek. "What! My God, where did you get all that money?"

Dad looked embarrassed. "Actually, the father of my roommate at prep school had a charge account there."

"Aha," Mom said. "The plot thickens."

"It was a triple date," Dad said. He took the sauce off the stove.

"Was it blind all around?" Mom asked. "Or just for you?"

"I can't remember."

The Stork Club is a fancy nightclub like the Copacabana. It's hard to imagine Dad going to a nightclub. "Did you dance?" I asked.

"Uh huh . . . And we drank champagne."

"This isn't fair," Mom said. "Here I was schlepping through the subway with Sylvester Lieberman and you were sipping champagne at the Stork Club!"

Dad just smiled.

"What was your first date like?" I asked. "I mean, the two of you."

Mom sighed. "Oh Lord, we went to that awful Irish play."

"It wasn't awful," Dad said.

"Deirdre of the Sorrows," Mom said. "That was it. Everyone was keening all through it."

"It was lyrical," Dad said. He poured some sauce on my ice cream for me. "Then we went out to eat."

"Em, this was really funny," Mom said. "Dad told his college roommate, Henry, that he was dating a Jewish girl and didn't know where to take her. So Henry said to take her to this dairy restaurant called Moskowitz and Lupowitz. So Dad took me there and we had— what *did* we have?"

"Mon streudel," said Dad. "And that's not true. I didn't say anything of the kind to Henry. I'd just heard it was a good restaurant."

"What's mon streudel?" I asked. It sounded yucky.

"It's this strange thing they make with poppy seeds," said Mom. "Dad was sure I had practically grown up on it, and in fact I'd never even tasted it."

Dad was smiling. "Remember my hat?" he said.

"How could I forget?" Mom said. To me she added, "Dad wore this hat when he came to pick me up . . . a real hat, you know, with a

103

brim and everything. But he put it in the back of my closet and when he left he forgot it. He never wore a hat again.''

"It's probably still there," Dad said. "I hope someone got some use out of it.''

I scraped up the last of my chocolate sauce. "But then did you know you wanted to marry each other right away?''

"No," Mom said. "We weren't even in love, at that point.''

"You weren't?" I was surprised.

"No," Mom said. "Were we?" she asked Dad.

"We were infatuated," Dad said.

"I remember I ran into Henry on the 86th Street subway and he said, 'I think he has a yen for you.' ''

Dad smiled at Mom. "He was right," he said.

Having a yen for someone is a strange expression. I wonder if it has anything to do with the Japanese money yen. I guess Tanner has a yen for me. I'm not sure if I have one for him, though.

I got sort of dressed up for the date. I shaved under my arms which is something I should do more often, but I always forget. Mom and Dad got me this electric shaver for Christmas, but then I lost the cord. I don't like to use the regular one Mom has. I'm afraid I'll cut myself. Mom said I could borrow this very nice embroidered Mexican blouse Dad got her for her birthday. She also said I could borrow a piece of her jewelry if I wanted to, so I did. I borrowed a pair of purple heart-shaped earrings and a small gold pin shaped like a fish. Mom has strange jewelry, lots of animal things and lots of things in bright colors. She said none of it is that expensive except the garnet locket Grandma gave her. It opens up and she has a tiny photo of Dad inside. Then I put on some of her Violettes de Toulouses perfume, just a little because it's really strong. I decided to wear my bra, finally. I got this bra with Mom about two months ago, but I never wear it to school. It's a one size fits all. I was sort of embarrassed when I went with Mom to get it. I kept being afraid I'd meet someone from school. "Just tell them you're shopping with your mother who's getting her first bra at forty," Mom said. "Say she's a little retarded." But we didn't meet anyone, in the end.

I think I have a good figure so far. I guess I might be very tall someday since I'm already five-feet-three and I'm only twelve. I wouldn't mind being five-feet-six or eight, but I hope I'm not over six feet. That would be *too* tall. Mom says I'm lucky in that I haven't gone through any awkward phases physically. I've never been very fat *or* very thin, just sort of in between. My breasts are okay too, not too big and not too small. My only trouble is that I have *huge* feet. Size nine! I couldn't believe it when I went to get boots last year. I definitely hope my feet won't get any bigger.

I wore these tan jeans I have and just knee socks and sneakers. I have one pair of shoes that are a little fancy, sandals, but since we were going bowling I decided sneakers would be okay.

I washed my hair and curled it with my Crazy Curl. Some of the curls looked a little crazy— they went up to the side—but basically they were okay. Then I put on some lip gloss that I got with Nicole at Gimbels East. I rubbed a little lipstick on my cheeks the way Mom does to make them look rosy. I looked pretty good.

When I came out, Mom and Dad were in the den. Most people use their living room a lot but we don't since Dad likes to work at his desk and Mom likes to be in the same room with him when he does. Olivia was sitting on the floor. Mom likes to play a game with Olivia that she made up. Mom sits on the floor around six feet away from Olivia and rolls the ball to her and Olivia rolls it back. Once, Mom went to answer the phone and when she got back she couldn't find the ball. She looked all over for it and then Olivia got up—she was sitting on the ball. She likes to trick people that way. I know she likes it because she gets a kind of gleam in her eye.

Dad was sitting at his desk. Dad's desk is sort of messy. He has lots of piles on it—piles of scientific journals, piles of letters he hasn't opened and stuff like that. Mom says sometimes she sneaks in and neatens up the piles, but basically she feels it's his right to be messy if he wants. Mom's studio is very neat. She has all the stuff she uses for her wall hangings in big boxes with colored labels on them. Mom says she used to think artists were supposed to be messy and she felt like she couldn't be a true artist because she's neat. But now she says she thinks being neat is okay, as long as you're not obsessive about it.

Actually, I think Mom *is* obsessive about it in certain ways. If I come home from school and take off my sneakers and leave them in the den, she always says, "Put your sneakers away." Or if I just drop my coat on my bed, she says, "Hang up your coat." The worst way she's like this is about my room. She won't let me hang up posters of rock stars. I used to and then we had the apartment painted and she tore them down. She said she *had* to tear them down because of the painters, but I happen to know that's not true. She tore them down because she hates them. She says Andy Gibb and Elton John are ugly which is simply not true. She says they should cut their hair or at least brush it which I think is very prejudiced. But mostly she says she thinks an apartment is an aesthetic expression of a person's taste and she wants my room to have really nice artistic posters by real artists like Andy Warhol or Chagall. It's true, the posters in my room are nice, but I still don't think it's fair that I can't put up posters of Andy Gibb and Billy Joel. Nicole has around a hundred posters in her room! Mom would really freak out if she ever saw it. She says when I go away to college, I can live like a pig and put up all the rock posters I want, but right now I have to do what she says.

"Wow!" Dad said, turning around. "You're going to knock them dead."

"Thanks," I said.

"The top looks nice on you," Mom said. Mom borrows my clothes sometimes so it's fair if I borrow hers. The only trouble is, her hips are bigger than mine so we can only trade tops, not pants.

"When is the gentleman caller due to arrive?" Dad asked.

"At seven," I said. I sat down and began rolling the ball to Olivia.

"What's his name?"

Dad is like that. I've told him about ten times what Tanner's name is, but he doesn't listen! "Tanner," I said.

"Tanner? What kind of name is that? Does his father stretch deer skins?"

"His real name is Richard," I said.

"So, why doesn't he call himself Richard?"

"Sweetie, you don't realize," said Mom. "No one is called Richard any more. They all

108

have these weird names like Jupiter and Mace and Désirée . . . All the Judys and Barbaras and Richards and Davids are long gone.''

"We have a David in our class,'' I said.

"What does *he* call himself—Napoleon?'' Dad said.

"Daddy, come on! Please don't tease him about it or I'll kill you.''

Dad pretended to look shocked. "Never! What do you take me for?''

"What do we do with him, exactly?'' Mom said.

"What do you mean, what do you do with him?'' I asked.

"I mean, do we invite him into the front parlor and ask his intentions?''

Dad gave her a fishy glance. "Sweetie, this isn't 1890.''

"Just say hi, that's all,'' I said.

"What are your plans for the evening?'' Dad asked.

"We're going bowling,'' I said.

"I was terrible at bowling,'' Mom said.

"Em,'' said Dad, "there are two main things to remember—roll it hard. Get your arm back and really give it a heave. And keep your eye on the center of the pins.''

"Okay,'' I said.

Tanner came at ten past seven. He looked nice. He was wearing jeans and a T-shirt and a denim jacket. I hoped Mom wouldn't mind—

he has slightly long hair. Not really long, like Andy Gibb, but longer than Dad's.

I brought him in and introduced him to Mom and Dad.

"I think we met at the party," Dad said.

"Hi, Olivia," Tanner said. He just sort of stood there like he didn't know what to do or say.

"I think they say it's going to rain," Mom said. "Better take an umbrella, Em."

"Okay, I said. "I will."

Actually, my parents are okay. I think they make a pretty good impression on most people. I mean, they don't have any outstandingly weird traits.

The bowling was good. I did terribly, though. I tried to do what Dad said, aim down the middle, but I guess my aim isn't that good. It would just wobble off to the side. I got a score of around 45. Tanner was really good. He did what Dad said—he rolled it really hard. A couple of times he knocked down all the pins. I don't think I could ever do that.

After we were finished, we had something to eat. There's a place to eat right in the bowling place. I told him about how I wanted to be back by nine so I could watch *Pizzazz*. He said he'd be interested in watching it with me. I ordered a cheeseburger and a Coke. I didn't know if I should pay. I sort of believe in girls paying, but

I didn't know what to do. Anyway, it wasn't that expensive.

Tanner had a grilled-cheese sandwich and a Coke. He's a vegetarian.

"Do you mind if I have a cheeseburger?" I said.

He said he didn't. He said he just didn't believe in killing animals. Nicole is that way about women having fur coats. If she sees someone on the street in a fur coat, she yells something rude at them. I really should be a vegetarian too since I love animals, but the trouble is I love meat too. Imagine never being able to have lamb chops or steak again!

"I don't think I have the hang of bowling," I said.

"Well, you have to do it more," he said.

"Yeah." I took a big bite of my cheeseburger. "Basically, I'm not that good at sports, I guess."

"You're not so bad," he said, but I could tell he was just saying it to be polite. Actually, I don't care. I mean, there are lots of things I *am* good at, so I don't think it matters that much.

We had to hurry to get home in time for *Pizzazz*. Tanner asked if I'd been nervous being on TV. I said not as much as I expected.

Tanner said he thought maybe he would be a pianist when he grows up, but he isn't sure because he gets nervous when he has to perform. "My hands get all sweaty," he said. "I have to keep rubbing them on my jeans."

At home Olivia was asleep in her cage. Mom said that was too bad because then she wouldn't see herself on TV. I wanted to wake her up, but Mom said that wasn't fair.

It was interesting, watching us on TV. I wasn't bad. I had this funny expression some of the time, out of nervousness I guess, but Olivia was really good.

"That was nice," Mom said. "You were good, Em."

"Yeah, you were terrific," Tanner said.

Mom and Dad said they were going to turn in. I think they may have said that because they thought I wanted to be alone with Tanner. Tanner asked if I wanted to watch *Fantasy Island* which was on next. I said okay. While we were watching, he put his arm around me, just over the top of my shoulders. I didn't mind.

When it was over, I said I was a little tired and he said he was supposed to be home by midnight, anyway. He lives in Brooklyn which is pretty far away. I've never been there.

I walked him to the door. I had the feeling he would try to kiss me goodnight. He did. He sort of stood there for a while, looking nervous. Then he leaned over and kissed me quickly on the lips. It was okay, not that different from playing spin the bottle. He just took a little more time doing it. I told him I had a good time and he said we should do it again.

I guess Tanner would like it if I went out with him a lot, the way Sallie goes out with David. I don't think I want to, though. I mean, I like him, but I'm not madly in love with him or anything. It's weird to think that in a few years I might really fall in love with someone and make out with him, the way teenagers evidently do. I guess it's something that might be appealing if you really liked someone. Mom said she hardly went out with anyone in school; she was sort of a wallflower. Dad didn't either. He just went to these things called mixers where there are a lot of people you don't know. Mom says they were both "late bloomers." They didn't go out with that many people before they met each other.

I don't know if I'll be a late bloomer. I don't think so. I don't think I'll be an early bloomer, but not especially late. The trouble is I want someone who's really nice and smart and loves animals. Tanner is fairly nice, but he's not that smart. He does love animals, that's true. Mom says love isn't something you analyze, it just happens. She says you kind of look at someone and get carried away. Then, later, you find out you really like being with them and doing things with them. She says that's what happened with her when she met Dad. She was at this party and he was there and she went over and started talking to him. "I thought, where did this terrific guy come from?" she said. "I had to get smashed on about three glasses of this terrible punch before I had the courage to go up and talk to him." Dad didn't even ask for Mom's phone number when they first met! But he did ask his roommate, Henry, for it the next day.

I want to be like Mom and Dad. I don't want to get divorced. I want to meet somebody I can love for the rest of my life. So if I have to wait a long time before I meet that person, I will. I hope I won't have to wait *too* long, though.

Chapter 10

On Monday when I came home from school, Mom was there. Usually she isn't home till around five but I figured maybe she wasn't feeling well or something since she was lying down in the living room with a blanket over her. "Hi, Mom!" I said.

"Oh sweetie," Mom said, sitting up. "There you are. I'm glad to see you."

I wondered why she was so glad to see me when she sees me every day. "Aren't you feeling well?" I said, going into the room.

"No, I'm fine. I just felt a little tired."

"Where's Olivia?"

"She's inside, in her cage . . . Em?"

"Yeah?"

"Listen, something very . . . well, wonderful really has happened, and I just wanted to tell you about it."

I wondered what it could be. Maybe she'd

sold something for a million dollars and we were going to be really rich!

"I'm pregnant!" she said with a funny smile. "I'm going to have a baby!"

"You are?" I tried not to look disappointed.

"I just got the results of the test this afternoon."

"Oh . . . well, that's nice," I said without that much enthusiasm.

"Hon, I know it will take you awhile to get used to the idea," Mom said, "but, well, think how exciting it's going to be!"

"Yeah." I could think of at least a million more exciting things than having a baby!

At dinner Dad poured champagne for everybody. Mom had called him at the lab and told him.

"It's coming in October," Mom said. "I'll go see Gunderson next week."

"Who's Gunderson?" I asked.

"He's my gynecologist," Mom said. "He delivered you, Em."

"October's a good month," Dad said.

"What's good about it," said Mom, "is I won't be so terribly huge over the summer. It's such a drag being enormous in August."

"You were never that enormous," Dad said.

"I felt enormous," Mom said.

This is the thing that surprised me. I thought Mom and Dad only wanted one child. They're always saying how expensive children are and they both have careers and they *are* sort of old. I mean, Dad's forty and Mom's thirty-eight. Most people have children when they're in their twenties. That means, when this baby is my age, Dad will be fifty-two and Mom will be fifty. That seems awfully old to be parents. You'd expect people to be grandparents by then. Of course, I couldn't say that to Mom and Dad because that might hurt their feelings.

After supper I went into my room to do my homework. But I just couldn't concentrate. To tell the truth, I felt lousy which made me feel bad because Mom and Dad seemed so happy about the baby. The thing is, I enjoy being an only child. I don't think it's true, the way books say, that only children are spoiled and selfish and all of that. *I'm* not spoiled or selfish. It's one thing if you have a brother or sister who's two years younger or older than you are. Then you can play with them. But I'll be thirteen by the time this baby is born! I'll be practically like his or her aunt or something. Besides, we have Olivia. I don't see why we need a baby.

Mom came into the bathroom while I was taking a bath. I find that taking a long hot soapy bath makes me feel better when I'm feeling depressed.

"Mom, did you really want to get pregnant?" I asked.

"Sure," Mom said. "Lord, we've been

trying to have a baby since you were born, practically, Em.''

"You were?'' I wasn't sure what she meant by "trying.'' "What do you mean by trying?'' I asked.

"I mean, when Dad and I make love, I haven't been using any form of birth control,'' Mom said. "You see, I had these two miscarriages when you were little and the doctor wasn't sure I could get pregnant again.'' Mom explained that she had gotten pregnant twice and each time, when the baby was about three months old in her stomach, she would lose it. She said that made her feel just terrible.

"Were they boys or girls?'' I said. "The ones you lost?''

"One of each.''

That made me feel even worse, knowing I didn't especially want the baby when she wanted it so much. "What if that happens again?'' I said.

"Well, the thing is,'' Mom said, "this time I'm really going to take it easy. It goes against my personality, but I will. I'll take a cab to my studio and I'll even try to work sitting down if I have to. And I'm supposed to have a glass of gin every night.''

"How weird! How come?''

"I don't know. . . . It relaxes you, evidently. . . . Em, don't worry. It will change things, in a good way. I think you'll really like it, after a while."

"Sure," I said. I tried to smile up at her. "No, I'm really looking forward to it," I lied. I guess I might have been if we didn't have Olivia. I just don't see the *point* in a baby when we have one already, one that's so much nicer and smarter than any dumb *real* baby will be.

Mom looked like she knew I was lying. "I drank too much champagne," she said, looking at herself in the mirror. "I feel woozy."

That weekend I told Nicole about the baby.

"You mean they're still doing it?" she said. "Weird."

"Mom said they've been trying ever since I was born."

"I guess they really wanted one a lot."

I remember once I took this book on the uterus and things out of the library at school. Mom looked at it and then she said, "Em, this explains all about why people make love so they can have babies . . . but it leaves out that it's just something that's very enjoyable to do." She smiled. "Maybe Nature did that on purpose so there'd always be a lot of babies. She didn't know there'd be a population problem."

"I think they might do it anyway," I said to Nicole.

"Really?"

About six months ago a really embarrassing

119

thing happened that I've never told anyone about, not even Nicole. I was looking for this notebook that I'd left in Mom and Dad's bedroom so I went in there to get it. When I opened the door, there was Mom sitting on top of Dad. She wasn't wearing a thing! When Mom saw me, she let out a whoop and dove under the covers. Dad said in this calm way he has, "We'll be out in a minute, Em." Usually they lock the door. Sometimes, I've tried to go in and the door is locked and when Dad says, "We'll be out in a minute, Em," I know what that means. I mean, why shouldn't they do it? They're married, after all. I guess one reason you marry someone is you like to do it better with them than with anyone else.

It's just odd to think of your own parents doing it. Especially Dad. He's so calm all the time. I just can't imagine him doing it at all! Till I was about eight I never saw Dad without his clothes on. He always locked himself in the bathroom when he took a shower or anything. And I was really curious. I kept pestering him, saying I wanted to see him without any clothes on. Finally Mom took me aside and said that Dad had just been brought up in a more repressed home than she had and the idea of me seeing him without clothes on made him really embarrassed. She said she thought that I shouldn't keep bugging him. So I stopped bugging him, but I was still curious. Then one day when I was nine, Dad called me into their bedroom in this sort of embarrassed, formal way he has. He said he had decided it would be okay if I saw him naked. And he just took all his clothes off, right then and there! You could tell it was really hard for him to do it. I looked at him. It was interesting, but after that I didn't care that much. The funny thing is after that he stopped locking the bathroom door and if I'd come in while he was showering, he didn't seem to mind the way he did before, but I just wasn't that interested any more.

"Listen, all I'm saying is: watch out," Nicole said. "They'll do the same thing to you that mine did to me: force me to babysit."

"Mom said they'd pay me though. She said it would be like when I babysit for Olivia. If I turn down other babysitting things, I deserve to get paid."

"Hey, that's a good deal!"

"I wonder if Olivia will like the baby," I said. "Sometimes they say animals are jealous of babies."

"You mean, you're still going to keep her?" Nicole said.

"Sure, why *shouldn't* we keep her?" I couldn't understand how she could even *ask* that.

"Well, I don't know . . . Your apartment isn't that big. Won't they want to use the den for the baby?"

I hadn't thought of that. "Well, we can put the baby in the living room for a while," I said defensively. "Babies don't need actual rooms."

"Yeah, but after a while they do. They grow up, unfortunately."

"Why unfortunately? I would think that's when they'd at least be interesting."

"Oh sure, once they're six or eight, they're okay. But the worst of all is when they're two to six. Believe me. They're wild and they destroy everything in sight, they can't talk that well, they're dumb and they aren't even in school so they have all day to roam around wrecking every prize possession you have. Get a lock for your door, right away."

"Even before it's born?"

"You can't start too soon."

"But as babies they're not so bad?"

"Well, they're not terrific. Some are worse than others. The worst ones are the colicky ones. Teddy was like that. He screamed his head off every day from four to six."

"I hope ours isn't like that," I said, getting worried.

"Eventually they stop," Nicole said, "but while it's going on it's murder, I tell you."

"You had three of them!" I said, suddenly envisioning what it must have been like.

"I've been through the war," Nicole said, sighing. "I'm a veteran . . . No, listen, you'll survive. But life will never be the same again."

"It won't?" I said, dismayed.

"No," she said blithely. "Look, you had twelve good years and that makes you lucky. I only had three. Some people have only one and a half. . . . And in six more you'll be at college."

"True . . . but you said they didn't get good till they're six."

"They get better . . . I didn't say good."

"What'll Mom and Dad do then?" I said, suddenly concerned. "I won't be around to babysit for them."

"They'll cope," Nicole said. "Listen, they're the ones that want the little beast . . . so let them bring it up. It's their problem."

"True."

I hope that the baby won't be a hard baby, like Nicole says Teddy was. I know it's immodest to say, but I was evidently a very good baby. Mom says I almost never cried and I ate everything that was put in front of me and was very jolly. I was really a pig when I was little— I had at least twelve chins!

At dinner I said, "I bet Olivia will really like the baby. She can help me take care of it."

Mom looked at Dad. "Uh . . . Em, listen, this is something Dad and I have been meaning to talk to you about."

"What?" I said warily.

"About Olivia."

"What about her?"

"Well, Mom and I have talked about it," Dad said in his slow way, "and we basically feel, Em, that it's just going to be too difficult with Olivia *and* a baby."

"Why?" I said. I was so scared my voice came out in a squeak. "What's so difficult about it?"

"Well, you know, animals can get very jealous with babies and they can, perfectly inadvertently, be a menace."

"Olivia's not like that!" I said indignantly.

"That's just one thing," Mom said.

"What else is there?"

"Well, take just her size. Now chimps get pretty big. She's going to be nearly one hundred pounds one day. It's one thing to have a cute little chimp in our apartment—it's another to have a full-grown, one-hundred-pound adult chimp. That's a whole other story."

"But you knew that when we got her!" I said. "You knew she would get big!"

"And we also knew that someday we would have to give her away," Dad said.

"But you never said that!" I cried. "You never said we'd have to give her away."

"Darling, we made it clear right from the start that this was an experiment, something we'd try," Dad said. "We never said we were signing on for life. How could we? Chimps live to be forty years old. Did you expect Mom and me to be babysitting for her for the next forty years?''

Nobody spoke for a while.

"Hon, listen," Mom said. "We love Olivia just like you do. We're going to miss her too."

But the thing is, they *won't* miss her! Because they'll have the baby and they'll be drooling all over it and probably not even remember Olivia at *all*. "Are you going to just put her in some terrible zoo?" I said. "With all kinds of smelly apes that are dumb and swing around on bars all day?"

Dad smiled at me. "Sweetie . . . we will only give Olivia to the very best zoo in the United States. We will investigate the whole thing thoroughly. We want her to be happy and well cared for. Don't worry about that for a minute."

"But what if it's not in New York?"

"Then we'll send her to wherever it is."

"But then I won't be able to see her!"

"We can still visit her—in the summer, on vacations."

"But I want to visit her every day," I said.

Dad sighed. "Em, listen . . . Right now you love Olivia very much. That's great. But a lot is going to happen to you in the next ten years. You'll be going to high school, then to college, then maybe you'll get married, get a job . . . You won't even *want* to visit Olivia every day."

"I will!"

"Which would you rather?" Mom said. "Would you rather Olivia was in a smelly awful zoo where you could visit her all the time or a nice zoo where she'd be very happy and you could see her summers?"

I thought a minute. "A nice zoo," I said finally.

"That's what we want too," Dad said.

"But Dad, even if it's nice, she'll miss us. She's used to being with people. She won't like living with a bunch of chimpanzees. She's used to all her toys and everything."

"Em, it's true, it will be an adjustment for her, but maybe we can find a place that has a whole group of chimps that have been raised with people . . . That way she'd feel right at home. And after a year, if it's a really nice place and she's well treated, she'll feel right at home."

"Will she remember us?" I asked anxiously.

"Of course!" Dad said. "She'll remember us as long as she lives just as we'll remember her as long as we live."

"Okay," I said. I didn't feel like eating any more. I went over and lay down on the couch. Dad came over and sat down next to me.

"Sweetie, you know, I think Olivia has been happy with us and maybe would be indefinitely, but she *is* an animal after all. I think she needs to be with other chimps. She needs some space to roam around, she *needs* to climb trees. It wouldn't be fair to keep her cooped up in a New York apartment all her life. It's unnatural that she should have to wear clothes and diapers."

I know that's all true, but I still feel bad. I went into the den. Olivia was sitting in her cage, playing with her "Dressy Bessy" doll. Here she didn't even know what was going to happen! That made me feel terrible. There was no way I could tell her or prepare her. One day she'd just get on a plane and go somewhere else and she wouldn't even know we were coming back to see her in the summer. I wish so much I could talk to her and she could understand. That way she'd understand exactly what was happening and why and she wouldn't mind.

I took her out of the cage and she snuggled up next to me on the couch. She likes to lie on her back and have me rub her stomach, almost like a dog. "I love you, Olivia," I said softly.

She looked up at me like she did understand.

Mom has to rest a lot. She started to bleed a little bit. The doctor said he didn't think that was dangerous but to be on the safe side, he thought she ought to stay quiet.

She brought some stuff back from her studio and works on it sitting up in bed with all her boxes of colored wool around her. She says it isn't so bad. Dad does all the grocery shopping now and I help. I certainly hope Mom doesn't lose this baby like she did those other two, especially now that it's practically old enough to be born. Dad said the danger time will be over in six weeks. Once the baby is eight months inside the mother's stomach, even if it's born prematurely, it's big enough to live.

It's going to be a girl and she's going to be called Rosalind. Mom went to have this test done called amniocentesis to see if she was going to be a mongoloid or had anything wrong with her. When they do that test, they also find out if it's a boy or a girl. Some people don't like to know—they want to be surprised—but Mom and Dad said they wanted to know so the doctor told them.

I was really disappointed when I heard they were going to name her Rosalind. I had thought up all these great names: Samantha, Amanda, Crystal, Veronica, Jessica and Melissa. Dad said they all sounded like names for girls in long flouncy dresses who would live on Southern plantations. He explained that he and Mom wanted to name the baby after someone they admired. He said the baby would be called Rosalind after a woman scientist named Rosalind Franklin. She did something important about the crystal structure of DNA and Dad says she should have won the Nobel Prize. Well, I guess Rosie isn't so bad for a nickname. It's sort of like that Maurice Sendak special they had on TV, "I'm Really Rosie."

When Mom was in her fourth month, I went with her when she got some maternity dresses. She said the ones she had from when she was pregnant with me were too short. It was this very fancy place called Lady Madonna and the dresses were pretty expensive. It was odd seeing all these pregnant women trying things on. Some of them looked sort of strange. Even now Mom is big, but not enormous. If you just looked at her from the shoulders up, you couldn't tell she was pregnant. Some of these women looked pregnant all over, from top to bottom. When we came in the store, this person came over to us and said, "Which of you is looking for some dresses?" I know I look old for my age, partly because I'm tall. I can get into PG movies without any trouble at all. So maybe they thought I was one of the teenagers on that show Nicole and I watched. Mom doesn't look that old, but her hair is a little gray so maybe they thought she looked too old to be pregnant. "They're for me," Mom said. "My daughter is just helping me decide."

In the end Mom picked three: a dark purple one with little yellow flowers on it, an olive green pantsuit and a bright orange one with a shocking pink arrow pointing down with "BABY" written above it. Mom said all but the last one she thought she could wear, belted, after the baby was born. "You can wear the other one too," Dad said. "It will give people something to wonder about."

Dad says he is very cool, calm and collected this time around. He said that when Mom was pregnant with me, he was a nervous wreck and practically had labor pains himself. Mom is going to have the baby induced if it's not born at a special time because the doctor doesn't want to take any chances. It seems I was born very fast, in around two hours, and they're afraid Rosie might come in half an hour or something like that.

Chapter 11

We wrote to all the zoos in the United States practically, asking them to send brochures and describe their ape houses in detail.

The zoos we liked best were one in the Midwest and one in San Diego. Dad wrote to them and told them about Olivia. The one in the Midwest said they didn't need any more chimpanzees. They said their breeding program had been "spectacularly successful." But the San Diego Zoo said they would like to hear more about Olivia. The woman who wrote us, Esther Holm, said she was interested in training chimpanzees and had a special group there who were being studied part of the time.

"That would be perfect, Em," Dad said. "That way she'd be with other chimps who are smart and she wouldn't just forget everything you taught her."

Esther Holm wrote back that she was going

to be in New York in September and would like to meet us and Olivia then.

By the time she came, Mom was really huge. She was wearing her dress with the arrow saying "BABY" but even if she hadn't been you could have told she was pregnant. That's another thing. I wish I could tell Olivia that Mom was pregnant so she'd know what was going on and why we have to give her away. But I can't.

Esther Holm was nice. She was a little funny-looking. Her skin was sort of pockmarked and she didn't wear any makeup. She had very short blond hair. She really loved animals. She said she'd been a zoology major in college and had thought of doing the thing Dad does, but decided she wanted to work in a zoo instead. She said she'd written to all the zoos to see which one she liked best and had waited a whole year until there was an opening in the San Diego Zoo. She's from Chicago.

She was really nice with Olivia. She didn't rush over and try to grab her or anything. She just watched her and waited until Olivia came over to her. She talked to her in a nice, quiet voice.

"So, Olivia, how do you think you'll like Southern California?" she said. "Are you laid back enough?"

She said that, as an Easterner, she couldn't get used to how relaxed and casual everything was in California. "I'm racing around frantically the way I always have and everyone else is ultra cool and calm. I'm kind of a fish out of water." She said she really missed snow.

"I think Olivia will like it, though," Mom said. "The warm climate."

"Most of our chimps do. It's a dry heat, not uncomfortable."

"Could we visit her, though," I said, "when we go out there in the summer?"

"Of course," Esther Holm said. "I'm sure Olivia would be terribly disappointed if you didn't."

At the end Mom and Dad talked with her about when we should bring Olivia out there. Mom doesn't want to fly because Rosie is due so soon, and Dad doesn't want to leave Mom. So we decided I would fly out with Grandma and Grandpa at the end of September, just before school starts. That's two weeks from now.

After Esther Holm left, I started feeling really terrible. I know I shouldn't have because she was so nice and the zoo sounded so good, but I guess I suddenly realized that in two weeks Olivia wouldn't be living with us any more and never would, ever again.

"Sweetie, cheer up," Mom said. "Olivia's going to be very happy."

"Maybe in the end she will," I said, "but in the beginning she's going to think that we deserted her."

"Honey," Dad said. I thought he was going

133

to say: don't anthropomorphize. Instead he said, "Why don't you go in and call Grandpa and discuss the trip, okay?"

I did that. Grandpa said he would love to go. Grandma said she would love to except she's working on a series of ceramic plates for a friend who's getting married. Grandma makes ceramic things for a hobby, jewelry and plates and things like that. We have these cups she made that are really pretty. They have a kind of bluish-brown glaze on them.

It was really hot the day Grandpa, Olivia and I went out to the airport to fly to San Diego. We had had a tough time finding an airplane where they wouldn't make Olivia ride in the baggage car, but we finally did. Dad said Olivia was a "seasoned traveler," and wouldn't cause any problems. Olivia was just wearing this light yellow sunsuit. I wore jeans and a sleeveless shirt. I was really boiling. When it's really hot, I wear my hair in a pony tail, even though I like it better loose. Grandpa just wore a regular gray suit like he usually does, but in some light material.

On the plane Grandpa kept joking around with the stewardess. He introduced Olivia to her as his great-granddaughter. "This is my granddaughter and this is my great-granddaughter," he said. "Do you see any resemblance?"

"Grandpa, come on," I said. "Quit fooling around."

"This puritanical young lady thinks only the young can have any fun," Grandpa said. "I ask you: Is that fair? Is that just?"

Olivia had a Coke and I had ginger ale. Grandpa just had tonic water. I gave Olivia all my goldfish crackers and she ate them up. "Grandpa, is she going to be sad when we leave her?" I said.

"Sad?" Grandpa said. "Why should she be sad?"

"She'll miss us."

"Well, but she'll have lots of new friends and this Miss—"

"Holm."

"—this Miss Holm sounds like a very congenial person. I think Olivia will be just fine."

"We can go out and visit her," I said, "but that won't be till next summer!"

"I'll tell you what," Grandpa said. "You and me and Grandma will go out and visit Olivia at Christmas. We'll just fly out, the three of us, and we'll bring Olivia something she really wants for a Christmas present."

"Maybe a big bunch of bananas?" I said, feeling better.

"The biggest bunch you ever saw," Grandpa said. "The biggest and the best."

Christmas isn't that far away, just about three months. That made me feel better.

We took Olivia to the zoo in the morning. Esther Holm was there to meet us. She was wearing jeans and a short-sleeved blouse. "So, how did the three of you survive the trip?" she said.

"Okay," I said. I was beginning to feel awful again.

She showed us all around the zoo. It really was nice. The animals had lots of space and it was clean. "This is what all zoos should be," Grandpa said.

"It is," Esther Holm said, "but unfortunately it's not the way all zoos *are*."

She showed us the other pygmy chimpanzees that Olivia would live with. They looked nice. Some of them were bigger because they were older. "We'll start her out with just one or two other chimps," she said, "and let her ease into it. I think she and Maxine ought to get along."

"Which one is Maxine?" Grandpa asked.

"She's that little one over there . . . She's just about Olivia's age, about a year."

Finally we had to go. Our plane was leaving at noon. Esther Holm took Olivia in her arms. "See you at Christmas," she said. Grandpa had told her about how we were planning to come back then. She said she'd write and tell us all about how Olivia was doing.

"Goodbye, Olivia," I said. I bent over and kissed her, and gave her a hug. She put her arms around my neck like she wanted to climb into my arms. I had to pull away.

When I got into the cab I burst into tears. All

the way to the airport I cried and cried. Grandpa kept patting me on the shoulder. "Sweetheart," he said, "we'll be seeing her again in three months. The time will fly."

I tried to stop crying. "I know," I said, "but I still feel terrible."

On the plane there was this dumb movie about some subway being hijacked, but it was good because it did take my mind off Olivia. When we got off the plane in New York, I didn't feel good, but I didn't feel as bad as I had before.

Grandpa just slept through the whole movie! He says exciting movies put him to sleep.

Chapter 12

Esther Holm is so nice! She writes to me every month about Olivia and I write her back. Last week she wrote:

Dear Emmy,
Olivia is doing just fine. She and Maxine have really hit it off, just as I thought they would. They run all around, playing leap-frog and various games. They're really having a ball! I showed Olivia the big photo of you that you sent. Guess what she did? She snatched it from me and ran off with it to show it to Maxine! Now she won't let me have it back.

I'm glad Olivia liked the picture of me. I just sent it because I didn't want her to forget who I was. Not that I think she really would, but I wanted to make absolutely sure. It's only six weeks till Christmas. Usually I'm all excited about Christmas because of the presents I'm getting, but this year all I can think of is that we'll be flying out to San Diego and I'll see Olivia again. Mom and Dad said they would come too, with Rosie. It will be weird in some ways, having Christmas in a very warm place. I wonder if they have Christmas trees in California. It seems like it would be hard to celebrate Christmas that much in a warm place. It's like you really need it to be cold and snowy to get into the mood.

At Thanksgiving Grandpa told us wonderful news. His book is going to be published! He sent it to some publisher and they really liked it! They want him to change some little things, but not that much. Grandpa is so excited! And guess what? He's going to dedicate it to me. He said it's going to say: "To Emily, who read this book first and liked it before anyone else." He said he wanted to say "To Emily, my favorite and only granddaughter," but now he can't because of Rosie. I told him he better write another book and dedicate it to Rosie or she might get jealous. He said he would. He said maybe he would write a book about Olivia. That would really be good. I asked if it would be from her point of view, and he said no, because he didn't like that kind of book. He said maybe it would be her life story and he would use some of the photos we took of her.

I bet Olivia will love it when that book comes out. I'm going to bring her a copy and show her. I wonder if she'll remember all those times, like when she was in the park and that boy bit her or when she was sick.

The place Mom is having her baby at is called The Maternity Clinic. Dad said when Mom had me, he wanted to be with her and help because they took this class together on natural childbirth, but they wouldn't let him. So this time they picked a place where he can stay the whole time. He said I could stay too, if I want.

I said I'd come along and maybe watch and maybe not. The thing is, I am sort of squeamish about things like that. I've heard babies are all slimy and yucky looking when they're first born and there's blood and everything. Dad says it isn't like that and that it would be good for me to get over my fears about it. That's probably true, but I don't know if I'm going to watch.

Mom started having labor pains on Monday night. It was around ten o'clock. I was doing some homework and Dad was working at his desk. We were both in the den when Mom suddenly called out, "Phil!"

Dad rushed in and so did I. Mom was in bed. She said, "I think the bag of water just broke."

The bag of water is something they told me about, but I forget what it is. I think when it breaks, it means you're in labor, something like that. Dad called Dr. Gunderson right away and we rushed down to get a cab.

Dad seemed more nervous than Mom. His hands were icy cold and he looked sort of pale. Mom seemed just the same as usual, except once in a while she'd close her eyes and then open them and say, "Wow, that was a big one." She said those were contractions. That means the baby is pushing to get out.

When we got to the clinic, they took Mom into this room to get her ready. Dad heaved a deep sigh. "Well, we made it to the hospital," he said. I guess he'd been worried Mom would have the baby in the cab or something.

The doctor came out and said to Dad that Mom was "almost fully dilated" and that the baby would be born any minute.

Dad turned to me. "Okay, Em, this is it. Do you want to watch or not?"

"I don't know," I said.

"Well, make up your mind."

"I guess I don't want to."

I sat outside in this waiting room. I really am a coward. Maybe someday I'll have to have a baby and here I can't even face watching someone else having one. But I think watching it might be worse than doing it. I can't imagine being like those women Mom told me about who watch their own baby come out through special mirrors.

About twenty minutes later Dad came out.

"She's here! Want to see her, Em?" He looked all excited.

"Okay," I said.

I went into the room. Mom was lying there with Rosie on her stomach. She smiled at me. "How do you like her?" she asked.

I'd expected her to look absolutely awful so I wasn't that disappointed. She did look pretty bad, but not as bad as I expected. She wasn't all slimy—I guess they'd dried her off. The funny thing is she had bright red hair.

"How come she has red hair?" I said. Mom and Dad both have dark brown hair, like me.

"It must be from Grandma May," Mom said. "She was a redhead when she was young."

After a while the doctor said he thought Mom should rest a little while. He said she could go home tomorrow morning. By then it was three in the morning. "You two better go home and get some sleep," he said to us.

Dad and I took a cab home. We had a snack in the kitchen before we went to bed. I had hot chocolate with a marshmallow on top and Dad had a glass of beer.

"She was okay," I said. "She wasn't so bad."

"What I think you'll love," Dad said, "is when she starts to learn to talk. There's nothing on earth more fascinating than watching a human being acquire speech. It's an amazing thing."

142

"But that won't happen till she's two!" I said.

"No!" Dad said. "Babies start to talk way before that, not perfectly, but they start to try . . . Did I ever show you that record I kept of all the words you used to say?"

"No." I was really interested. Dad never even told me he did that.

"I'll show it to you in the morning," he said.

"Do I have to go to school?"

"No, let's both take the day off," he said. "Let's sleep as late as we want."

"Great," I said. I love sleeping late.

In the morning Dad showed me the book he kept about me. It was really interesting. I didn't start to talk much till I was one and a half, but after that I made up for lost time. I used to call anything round, like nuts or balls, "apples." For some reason I called bicycles "ca go" and photos "fo fo." When I was around two and Dad asked if I wanted to sit on the potty, I said, "No, I don't and I know it very well." Once I made a b.m. in my diaper and I said, "No bravo for that." Then I added, "Maybe a little bravo." I guess I was quite a witty child.

What I'm going to do is keep the same kind of record for Rosie that Dad kept for me, all her words and expressions and everything. Then, when she's big, I'll show it to her.

I feel a little bit guilty because it's true Olivia couldn't talk and that wasn't her fault—chimps just don't have the right vocal cords. It's not that I don't miss Olivia. I do. I think about her all the time. But I still think that maybe having a baby in our family will be interesting too in a different kind of way. I mean, I know it will be a long time before I love Rosie as much as I love Olivia, maybe never, but that's okay. Dad says the main thing is to be nice to her. He says you can't force love and you shouldn't try.

Chapter 13

On Christmas Day we drove out to Grandma and Grandpa's with Mush at around noon.

We're going to celebrate Christmas with Grandma and Grandpa and Mush, like we usually do, and then all fly the next day to San Diego.

Here are the presents I've gotten for everyone. I saved up my babysitting money so I could spend a lot. For Mom I got some special colored wools that I saw in a notions store near my school. They are really pretty and in the bright colors she likes: violet, yellowish green and turquoise blue. For Dad I got this frame which holds three photos. In it I put a photo of me, one of Mom and one of Olivia. I figured he could take it to the lab and put it on his desk. For Grandma I got a set of candlesticks since she like candles so much. They're made of a bubbly kind of glass. For Grandpa I got a little white plastic thing you can put clips and rubber bands and things like that into. He's always saying he wants to be better organized so that should help. For Mush I didn't know whether to get something to do with poetry or something to do with cooking. I decided on something to do with cooking since that was easier. I got him a gadget called a "Mr Lean Mr Fat Gravy Boat"; it helps you to pour gravy. I bought it at a store called Hammacher Schlemmer that has all sorts of weird things like that.

For Rosie I got a set of rubber dinosaurs. I guess she won't appreciate them till she's a little older, but they're really good. They look like real dinosaurs. A little book came with them explaining what they were.

Rosie slept through most of the dinner. When she woke up, Mom gave her some squash and stuffing. She just fooled around with it, though. Mostly she still has bottles. Rosie looks quite good now, for a three-month-old. She has all this funny bright orange hair. Mom bought colored wool ribbons at Woolworth's and sometimes she ties one around to match whatever Rosie is wearing. I would say so far she's not as bad as I expected. Maybe it's good that what I expected was so bad, that almost anything would've been better. She's not as good as I was. She doesn't sleep as much and she does get fussy sometimes, but not like Nicole said

Teddy did, really howling. If you pick her up and carry her around, she stops. Of course, you don't always feel like doing that. Sometimes I carry her around the apartment and explain things to her. Like I'll say, "That's a painting Mommy and Daddy got of a giraffe. See? He has a long neck." I call them Mommy and Daddy for her. When she's older she can call them Mom and Dad. She might not understand everything I say or even anything, but then again she might. You just can't tell with babies. Sometimes she tries to talk. She puckers up her mouth and makes these funny sounds. I guess she is saying something, but I can't tell what. I bought a scrapbook to start keeping a record for when she starts to talk, but she hasn't said anything worth recording so far.

I got some good presents. From Mom and Dad a skirt and blouse. It's true, I never wear skirts and blouses, but Mom thought I should have one, just for fancy occasions, like if I go to a play with her in the evening or something like that. It's dark blue and the blouse is bright yellow with flowers on it. Grandma made me a ceramic bowl to put things in. It has a nice glaze, like on those cups she made for us—sort of a soft blue color. Grandpa gave me a big beautiful book on apes with lots of huge color photos. I bet it was really expensive. Mush gave me something unusual. He wrote all the poems of his I like best and tied them together in a book. Each poem is on a different color page. He used to study something called calligraphy so each poem is written in very fancy script, the way they used to a long time ago. Mom always says she thinks handmade presents are the best.

"Are you excited about seeing Olivia again?" I asked Mush. We were sitting in front of the fire. Mom and Dad were swimming in the pool. Dad got Mom a new bathing suit for Christmas. It's red with white spots. It's a lot better than her old one. Rosie was sitting in her infant seat.

"Very," Mush said.

"I'm excited," Grandpa said. "I can scarcely contain myself."

For Olivia's present we got the biggest bunch of bananas you ever saw. It must have around twenty bananas on it. They all look good, pure yellow with no spots or anything. I hope Olivia shares them with her friends because if she doesn't, they might spoil before she can eat all of them.

When Mom and Dad got out of the pool, I played a piece with Grandma. Mush accompanied us on his recorder. He's very good at the recorder even though he didn't even start playing it till he was around twenty-two!

"Olivia likes music," I said. "Maybe we can play something for her."

We flew out to San Diego at two the next day. Grandpa had made reservations for us at this really fancy hotel. Grandpa likes fancy hotels. He likes room service. I do too. It's fun to call up and get anything you want. I even had my own room, right next to Mom and Dad's. Rosie stayed with Mom and Dad. Mom said she thought it was slightly decadent to stay in such a fancy hotel, but Dad said she should relax and enjoy it.

I was really scared when we went to the zoo in the morning. What I was scared about was that Olivia might not recognize me. I did send her my photo and Esther said she seemed to like it, but I was still scared.

Esther Holm met everybody and admired Rosie. I guess people feel they have to say a baby is cute, but Rosie really *is* cute. She's also really rosy. She has big, bright pink cheeks just like babies in pictures. I had tried to explain to her about the zoo and about Olivia. I showed her all the photos in my scrapbook of Olivia and also the book Grandpa got me. "That's an ape," I said, "and that's a chimp. That's a chimp we know. She's practically a member of our family."

"There she is," Esther Holm said. We looked out and there was a group of chimps under a tree. I could tell which one was Olivia right away.

"Which one is Olivia?" Mush asked.

"She's the one in the middle," I said.

Esther Holm brought Olivia over to us. She

wasn't that different, not that much bigger than three months ago. When she saw us, she began to hoot as loud as she could. Then she jumped right into my arms! I was so excited.

"Emmy was afraid Olivia would forget us," Dad said, smiling.

"Not a chance," said Esther. She said she would distribute the bananas around to all of Olivia's friends. That ought to make her very popular.

We stayed in San Diego a week. Every day I would go to the zoo with Grandpa. Grandma usually went with Mom and Dad and Mush to do sightseeing. Sometimes we'd take Rosie and sometimes they would. Esther Holm let us take Olivia out on walks. We would bring a picnic lunch and sit under a tree with her. Grandpa always brought her special treats, like pignolia nuts. She seemed to like them a lot.

I'm so glad she didn't forget me. This time I don't think I'll mind leaving her so much because I know she'll remember me. In the summer I can come and see her every day. Esther Holm said there's a special program for teen-agers who want to learn how to work with animals. That's what I want to do. I decided I don't want to be a veterinarian after all. I want to be someone like Esther Holm or Jane Goodall who studies chimps. That's what I'm going to do after I get out of college.

I think Olivia and Rosie like each other. At

first I think Olivia thought Rosie was some kind of doll. Rosie was sitting in her infant seat and Olivia came over and touched her arm. I thought Rosie might be scared, but she began to make these sounds she makes when she's excited. Then Olivia began to make *her* sounds. Maybe they could each understand what the other one was saying. If that's true, I wish I could be a baby because I'd love to talk to Olivia. I'd love to ask her how she likes it at the zoo and whether she misses us and all of that.

One day I brought my cello and I played her two new pieces I learned since she moved away: Saint-Saëns' *Allegro Appasionata* and Mendelssohn's *Song Without Words*. Olivia sat there and listened and so did Rosie, who was in her infant seat.

"Bravo!" Grandpa said when I was done. Grandpa loves to yell "Bravo!" He did that when I went to the opera with him once. I guess the people on the stage like it, but it was sort of embarrassing. People kept looking at us.

"Olivia, when we come back in the summer, I'll know a lot more pieces," I said. "I'll play them all for you . . . Do you think I could teach her to play the cello, Grandpa?"

"I doubt it," Grandpa said. "You could try, though."

"El," Rosie said.

151

I looked at her. "Grandpa!" I said. "She was trying to say 'cello.' Did you hear?"

"A most remarkable young lady," Grandpa said.

I felt really proud of Rosie. "Rosie's learning to talk," I said to Olivia. "Isn't that great?"

But then I realized that Olivia could never learn to talk; I didn't want to make her feel jealous. I cuddled her up next to me. "You're just as good as a baby," I said. "Don't you be jealous. You're every *bit* as good. You're the best chimp that ever lived."

She is, too.

ABOUT THE AUTHOR

Born in New York City, Norma Klein graduated from Barnard College with a degree in Russian, and later received a master's degree in Slavic languages from Columbia University. She has published numerous short stories, adult novels and books for young readers, including *Hiding*, *Naomi in the Middle*, *What It's All About*, and *Tomboy*, which are available as Archway Paperbacks. She received the "Child Study Children's Book Committee at Bank Street College Award" for *What It's All About*. Ms. Klein lives in New York City with her husband and their two daughters.

GROWING UP...
You Can't Run Away
from It and
You Don't Have To!

29982 HIDING $1.75
Norma Klein
Krii, shy and withdrawn, copes by "hiding"—until she meets Jonathan, who helps her come out of her shell. "Tremendous appeal."—West Coast Review of Books

42062 FIND A STRANGER, SAY GOODBYE $1.95
Lois Lowry
Natalie is haunted by a missing link in her life—the identity of her real mother—so she sets out on a journey to find her. "A beautifully crafted story which defines the characters with a full range of feelings and emotions."—Signal

42449 THE CHEESE STANDS ALONE $1.95
Marjorie M. Prince
Daisy takes a stand for independence as she begins to see herself in sharper focus through the eyes of the intriguing man who paints her portrait. "Absorbing." —Publishers Weekly

42450 CLAUDIA, WHERE ARE YOU? $1.95
Hila Colman
Claudia feels suffocated by her family, and runs away to New York City to find some kind of meaning in her life. "...presents a thought-provoking view of a current social problem."
—English Journal

29945 LETTER PERFECT $1.50
Charles P. Crawford
The story of three friends caught up in a blackmailing scheme. "Hard-hitting portrait of teenagers in crisis."
—Publishers Weekly

41304 THE RUNAWAY'S DIARY $1.75
Marilyn Harris
Fifteen-year-old Cat is on the road—in search of herself. "Believable and involving." —A.L.A. Booklist

44238 GROWING UP IN A HURRY $1.95
Winifred Madison
Karen discovers she is pregnant and must make a painful decision. "A hard-hitting and brilliantly written novel."
—Publishers Weekly